The Fantastic Strange

...so that it is all made plain...

VdA

The Fantastic Strange

Daniel Von der Ahe

Prism Press

This book is a work of fiction. Names, characters, places and incidents are either a product of the author's imagination or used fictitiously. Any resemblance to actual events or locales or persons, living or dead, is entirely coincidental.

The Fantastic Strange

For information on the art and prints visit:
www.thefantasticstrange.com

Prism Press

First Printing, 2016

ISBN 978-0-9970066-5-0

To Vincent, my father, whose support, interest, and patience have allowed me to discover who I am, and from whose example I have learned much and continue to do so.

Contents

Prologue

ACT ONE
The Plains

I	The Plains	17
II	The Whistle	32
III	The Train	35
IV	The Great Mephisto	44
V	The Mermaid	56
VI	The Arrival	66

ACT TWO
Before The Show

I	Karl The Strong	71
II	The Falconess	80
III	The Lady	84
IV	The Gypsy	95
V	The Wolfman	103
VI	Ivan	108
VII	The Serenade	112
VIII	The Marionette	118
IX	The Giant	126
X	Medina	138
XI	Heinrich's Dilemma	151

ACT THREE
The Show

I	The Fantastic Strange	157
II	Heinrich's Second Dilemma	165
III	The Butterfly	168
IV	Medina's Act	177
V	Judgment	184
VI	The Storm	192
VII	So Much Pain	198
VIII	The Masked Man	204
IX	Heinrich Speaks	220
X	So Much Wonder	229

ACT FOUR
After The Show

I	Gold	233

Epilogue

List Of Paintings

I	Creation	9
II	The Figurehead	13
III	The Camp	23
IV	A Train	37
V	The Docks	51
VI	The Beast	59
VII	The Grotto	65
VII	Rehearsal	75
XII	The Painted Lady	77
X	Karl The Strong	79
XI	The Falconess	81
XII	The Caravan	89
XIII	The Bearded Lady	93
XIV	A Curious Child	97
XV	Leonora The Gypsy	101
XVI	The Wolfman	105
XVII	Masquerade	111
XVIII	The Mermaid	113
XIX	Master Tack	121
XX	The Giant	125
XXI	Campfire	129
XXII	Quicksand	131
XXIII	The Giant Battle	133
XXIV	Imprisoned	135
XXV	Medina	141

XXVI   An Elopement   143
XXVII   Pirates   145
XXVIII   The Plank   149
XXIX   A Warning   153
XXX   The Great Mephisto   161
XXXI   The Cavewoman   163
XXXII   Winter In A Tent   169
XXXIII   The Show Goes On   173
XXXIV   A Siren Song   175
XXXV   The Gamble   179
XXXVI   Rabar   185
XXXVII   Stabbed   187
XXXVIII   All Is Ruin   203
XXXIX   Suicide   215
XL   She Went Wild   219
XLI   The Spirit Of The Universe   228
XLII   Gold   237
XLIII   Judgment   243

*"Before 'who,' ask 'what' I am. I am human.
And that is great. Otherwise, it all is ruin."*
-The Great Mephisto

*"Perhaps everything terrible is in its deepest being something
helpless that wants help from us."*
-Rainer Maria Rilke

"Have a wonderful time."
-Author

Prologue

In a time now fading, on a faraway sea, beyond the flight of the albatross, an old man gripped the railing of a crow's nest and tried to let go. *Do it,* he willed. *Let free.* He glared at the blotchy skin of his hands as they lifted from the railing. *Good.* His toes nudged over the edge of the rickety perch. A jumble of sails, yards, and lines crisscrossed below, obscuring his view of the distant deck. With a slight shift in the ship's direction, the main yard beneath him groaned as it angled for the wind. An opening between the ropes and canvas appeared. *End it,* he urged. *I've done my time.* A wind whipped his tattered breeches and his knobby knees shook. Sweat dripped into his eyes and blurred his vision. Suddenly, the deck began to rush at him and he lurched back against the mast, dizzy. *Coward!* he screamed inside. *Do you want to leave it up to fate?*

He fumbled for his telescope, directed it down to the front of the ship and adjusted the focus. Before the bow, the ragged figure of a man swayed in rhythm with the anchor chains. A diet of naught but salt water for months had left only a skeleton, bleached by the sun, with bits of sinew stubbornly holding the joints together, and naked, discounting the leather belt that hung from its spine and the few scraps of cloth that draped from its ribs. Salty black hair dangled grossly from its skull which was positioned to stare ahead with hollow eye sockets long since pecked clean. At certain headings, the wind blew just right and a haunting tune whistled through the dead man's broken teeth. *At least I cannot hear that death song from here,* the old man thought.

For six days, that prisoner had managed to survive his position, lashed to the bow and taking the brunt of each crashing swell, longer than any had done before. His perseverance had astounded the old man, but ultimately it had only served to prolong the prisoner's agony and the entertainment for the pitiless crew, all of them scoundrels. *He would have been better off giving up on the first day,* the old man reckoned. *Why endure the torture? Why the struggle?* Before the prisoner's soul had even left the body, nature, heedless, anticipating the end and hurrying it forth, had wasted no time in reclaiming her resources, and sent her variety of unrelenting scavengers to the task. Salt, wind, and rot had ravaged the prisoner's body and its state became more gruesome each day. The crew witnessed these injuries with sick fascination, and to their delight, upon noticing some thrashing, had twice discovered a shark pulled from the water by its appetite, its jaws locked on the body until the flesh had fallen free. The old man had witnessed one of those occurrences and shuddered to recall it still.

From the sea, we've come, and to it, return. What is the use of this cruel mess in between? The sailor stepped forward and re-gripped the railing. Once he'd dreaded this position and had struggled to hang on. Now he felt comforted by the isolation as he struggled to let go, but the rocking made it hard to determine when to do so. The smallest swell below caused the crow's nest to sway several yards one way, like an upside-down pendulum, and as far in the other. It hovered directly above the deck for only brief moments. With that brief window and the momentum of his swaying, he couldn't be sure he would hit the deck if he jumped. *It is just too hard to time just right.* He'd lost his other telescope trying to estimate the fall. When it splashed into the sea, he'd confirmed that dropping into the ocean would not be a dramatic or instant enough end.

A knotted scarf protected his scalp from the scorching sun as his hair had long ago abandoned this duty; it seemed to have gone to thicken the ranks of the white beard guarding his cheeks and jaw against windburn. A loose linen shirt billowed, unlaced from angular shoulders, revealing a chest as wrinkled as the garment itself, but roasted a honey brown where the shirt was bleached white, making the scribbles of faded, blue tattoos almost impossible to decipher. A black flag above his head snapped and brushed past his neck, but he didn't so much as flinch. He was used to it teasing him. *Yes, I know. I am a coward*, he minded. Stitched on the flag, the design of a skull framed by crossed bones unfurled and leered in the breeze.

The old man watched the sun bow to the soft bedding of clouds resting upon the edge of the sea, and as its golden crown cast a nostalgic glow across the sky, he realized he'd let another day pass without taking the opportunity to end it all. He hung his head and breathed a sigh past his creased lips. His watch was over and he would have to leave his post, one of the few places on the ship where he felt at ease. Alas, unable to jump, he would have to climb down defeated, and suffer the terrors of his life once more. As though to remind him of the wretchedness that awaited him below, shouts of the crew echoed up from the deck.

"Set the sails harder ye weaklin' or I shall scrape the barnacles with ye! If I've to do it meself, then to the sharks with thee."

"I've poor wenches in every port pinnin' for me wit broken hearts."

"Gift me here tha' bottle ye sloppy sinner 'fore I gut ye."

Sometimes he'd hear the ring of sabers being drawn. Usually, after a few bloated boasts and impotent threats were exchanged—rarely actual blows—the weapons returned to their belts. *Wretched little men*, he thought, though they weren't so little up close. *If only I could make the drop*. He imagined his body falling one hundred and forty feet, crashing through the decks and clean through the hull. He was the only man aboard able to repair such damage, and as he would be no more, the ship would be as good as sunk. In one fell fall, he could put everyone out of their misery.

Turning the telescope around, he looked through the larger end, postponing his inevitable descent. The ship looked even smaller beneath him, isolating him further. His breath fogged the glass and evaporated. *How did I get here?* he pondered as he had done so many times before.

From the beginning, he'd always been aimless. He'd not met his father, and so he'd had no immediate role model to guide him. His mother's family had been well-off, so he hadn't been forced by desperation to pick a career, though he did want to do something. He'd never discovered a natural talent for anything useful that might focus his energies, and his interests had been fleeting, never inspiring a passion. So, aimless he'd remained and, at the age of twenty, he'd chosen a rather aimless path. He took a job aboard a ship because, at the least, it promised the opportunity to explore, which is good for someone who has not yet found what he is looking for. He hoped his life's calling might just be hiding in a different place.

By chance of a vacancy, he'd become apprenticed to the ship's carpenter. Pleased to have a skilled position, he'd never asked what had happened to the other apprentice but soon realized that he probably should have. Following an unexpected series of explosions, cannon balls hurtling through the hull, and the discovery of his master's hands removed by a soldier's cutlass, came his realization of the piratical nature of his ship.

He'd trembled in shock for days after that first raid and been unable to decide whether it was more dangerous to stay or leave. During that time the captain had coaxed him to take the newly opened position of master carpenter, mostly by qualification of still having hands, and he'd been too rattled to refuse. That was fifty years ago.

For fifty years since, too cowardly to leave, he'd bent his back, blocked his ears, swung his hammer, and ignored the crimes of the crew. *Now my neck is crooked, my back is crooked, and my life is crooked,* he thought. He folded the telescope, secured it to his belt and took a last look at the reddening panorama and wondered, *all my life I have only served to keep a wretched ship afloat. Was there really nothing more?*

The breeze died down. The waves blended together like a lavender sheet spreading out on a bed. He looked at his disgraceful, gnarled fingers. *Too late,* he grieved. *What else can you do?* He slumped down, clenched his hands and struck the weathered railing. *It was all for naught, and pretty much no good. I give up.*

Looking into the sky, he whispered,

"Why me?"

A tear rolled down his face. His tongue darted out and nabbed the salty drop of despair. He began to wipe his cheek, but then gave up and just let the tears soak his beard. Suddenly, something jerked his attention away from his misery. A colorful sparkle flashed in the water off the starboard bow. He cleared the tears from his eyes. A large scaly tail flipped out of the foam. The carpenter sprung up and almost lost his footing. He grabbed a line, stepped onto the railing and leaned out until he was nearly perpendicular to the mast. Sure enough, an emerald green tail glittered just below the surface of the water, but it was unlike any he had ever seen before. He whipped his telescope out again and slammed it against his eye as he uttered,

"As I am a soul!"

The front half of the fish looked to be the torso of a human woman. A copper red mane streamed from her head. A mermaid if ever there was one. The rope slipped in the carpenter's sweaty hand. He flailed and

wrapping the rope around his wrist, held on for glorious life. *Don't let go now fool hands!* he screamed inside over his pounding heart.

He pulled himself back into the crow's nest and began to determine the swiftest route down. He entertained the idea of jumping again but decided it was too uncertain that he could catch the mermaid that way, and dangerous! A slightly safer option, though not as fast, he could slide and swing down lines, but he had not been young enough to do that for a long time. The last option, he could clamber down the rigging he had clambered up in the first place. He looked up from these options to pinpoint the mermaid again and gasped. The mermaid was gone.

No! He searched for any movement, just one more splash, but it was to no avail. He began to descend the rigging, slipping as he paid attention to the darkening waters rather than footholds. *How could she just vanish?* he pined. In his desperation, he considered that he had gone mad and the mermaid was just a delirium induced phantasm or a dream his old mind had concocted to assuage his sorrows. He brought his palms to his face and let them slowly drag down his coarse cheeks as he lamented in the wind,

> *"Alas, I have gained a feeling that is bound to drive me mad,*
> *A loss where I had none before, for something that I never had."*

That evening the carpenter tossed and turned in his hammock, but not because of the swaying ship or the rolling sea. His eyes kept snapping open in the dark, only to find pale moonbeams slanting through cracks in the deck. He was used to the creaks and groans that seemed to only come out at night and knew it could not be them that kept him awake. The mystery of the mermaid swam through his mind. He kept asking himself if it had been a coincidence that she'd appeared right after he'd given up and if she was some sort of sign. Preferring the idea that she had been a sign, he became inspired, rolled from his hammock, and lowered his toes to the floor.

He tiptoed between the hammocks pregnant with evildoers emitting fitful snores, and lowered himself down a deck via a short ladder. Finding his way in the dark, he entered his workshop and closed the door behind him, thankful he'd greased the hinges, and felt for his oil lamp. After lighting the lamp, he began to clear the deck of shavings and tools, and his mind cleared of questions as a plan took shape. He searched the shadowy recesses of the hold and located a block of beech as tall as himself. He hauled it into the light and began to mark it with a pencil and a chisel.

During the days that followed, he never let on about the project in his workshop. He replaced belaying pins, spliced ropes and tarred breaches in the hull to both keep the ship afloat and to show that he was working. The punishment for idle hands was the agony of the lash, but he now had the added concern that if caught flagging and subsequently flogged, his nightly endeavor would be more difficult to complete, for it is hard to work with a lacerated back. It was hard enough working through his lack of sleep. Through the daytime, he stumbled like a zombie and struggled to keep his eyes open, but he would not stop working through the nights, even when some mornings he awoke with his face in a pile of sawdust. For as he chipped away at the hardwood, sweating in the dank nights, he'd never felt more alive. He hummed tunes he'd forgotten for fifty years—songs he'd heard natives sing while dancing on tropical shores.

He couldn't stop, regardless of the risk of staying up all night and getting no sleep. At last, the point of his chisel peeled away the final curling sliver of pale wood. He sanded the refinement and brushed on a layer of paint. Stepping back, he raised his chin, rubbed his dusty beard and paced around the piece as sawdust blew from his nostrils.

This is why! he thought, answering the question he had asked right before seeing the miraculous mermaid. Then he covered his creation with a stretch of canvas, wrapped it with rope, and quietly left his workshop. He crept onto the main deck and was encouraged by the absence of the moon. Fresh salt air chilled his sweat-drenched body as it blew away the odors of rot and mold from the ship. The sound of that air rushing through the lines and the water crashing the keel reminded him of the wildness of nature and that she does not sleep. She is always ready. Above him, on the aftcastle, silhouetted against the faint illumination of stars, an angry lad named Williams gripped the helm. Below Williams, on the quarterdeck, his older, fatter brother lay against the bulwarks, a bottle gripped in his hand and drool sopping his vest. As long as they did not look down, the carpenter might accomplish his task, so he hoped. But he had no time to lose as the night had begun its retreat. A soft blue glow threatened at the edge of the

I Creation

sky. He hesitated.

Wait no more! he commanded himself.

He lifted open a hatch amidships on the main deck then rushed below and opened another hatch between two snoring hammocks. *Dream your dreams of war and thievery,* he thought. *Just keep dreaming tonight!* Down another deck, in his workshop, he hooked rigging to his carving and scampered up to the main deck again. Crouching at the edge of the hatch, he began to hoist his carving out. The enshrouded carving lifted off the low deck and rose past the swaying hammocks like a massive dark ghost. The hammocks swayed to the right and the heavy carving swayed to the right. The rope creaked and the carpenter held his breath. The hulking shape cleared the main deck, and he pulled his lines to the bulwarks, swinging a spar which flew the sculpture over the side of the ship. Then he lowered it over the bulwarks, out of sight, while carefully keeping it from being swept away in the waves.

If anyone discovered him now, he would say he was working on a repair. If questioned more seriously, he could release his creation into the sea before anyone noticed it, but he didn't want to find out if he'd be able to do that. He checked on the Williams brothers. Neither had moved an inch. Swiftly and silently the carpenter began to convey the sculpture towards the bow, tying one rope ahead as he loosed one rope behind. As the ship rolled, the sculpture swung towards him, coming within inches of crashing into the hull. Sweat drenched his back from his peril and exertions, as he tried to keep the ropes tight. At last, he secured the ropes, wrung his sore hands, and wiped his sopping brow. He was close and he knew it because he heard the eerie whistle singing clear and evil. How he hated that song of wind through a dead man's teeth. The blue on the horizon had grown lighter and glowed with a hint of pink. He had only a few moments before dawn, but it was now or all for naught; there was no going back. He clambered up to the bowsprit and began to shimmy forward, out over the waves, gripping lashings to avoid slipping as the hull punched the sea. Surging swells rushed up at him as the bow crashed low and salty spray drenched his face and blurred his vision.

With a grunt, he pulled himself, on his belly, to the point directly above the whistling skeleton and whispered,

"Now cease your ghastly song of blame,
Take to the depths our wretched shame."

He reached down with a sharp blade and slashed the bonds of the skeleton's ankles. As the skeleton swung forward, the carpenter slashed the bonds of its wrists, sending the prisoner flipping into a long overdue, watery grave. The moment the pathetic bones splashed into the crashing swells, the first rays of a ruby dawn spilled over the horizon, unrolling over the tumultuous sea like a rosy carpet to herald the flowering sun. *Too early!* The carpenter scooted back to the deck, careful to avoid slipping in his haste. He pulled a line through a block on the bowsprit, and with it he maneuvered his sculpture to the just vacated position of figurehead. When his sculpture settled into its post, the carpenter sighed. It fit perfectly. Just as he took in a deep breath and prepared to unveil it, a gust of wind impatiently swept in and snatched the sculpture's covering away, exposing the carpenter's carven creation to the world.

In place of the prisoner, a wooden mermaid, painted a pale cream, with cheeks and breast blushing to be so exposed, though it was due to the brilliant pink glow of the breaking day, now leaned forward with a lantern in her hand. Her hair, painted a copper red, was sculpted into two braids draping over her bare chest, which was thrust forward with all the confidence of a champion of hope. The carpenter, both pleased and fatigued, whispered to the brightening dawn as both he and the mermaid charged headlong towards it,

> *"Death, your reign is over. For me, it was not too late,*
> *You courted me when I was lost, but you were not my fate."*

II The Figurehead

Act One
The Plains

Chapter I
The Plains

Heinrich stopped on a slight rise. A half mile ahead, in a shallow valley, a few shanties stood haphazardly under a thicket of moss covered oaks. Thin clouds striped high in the early sky like white furrows in a far blue field. Bottlebrush and switchgrass swayed in a warm breeze and spread out in patches over the soft earth like a mangy hide. Pink blooms of the prairie smoke wildflower speckled the grasses. He cupped a blossom in his hand and recalled that he'd always thought it looked more like cotton candy than smoke. He was amazed by how many names and facts he still remembered about the nature around him. He had loved to study it as a boy but hadn't really paid it any attention for the last thirteen years; there wasn't a great deal of living nature in a coal mine.

He lifted his hat and pushed his fingers through damp, thinning hair. It felt good to have his sweat cooled by the breeze. It also felt good to be in the middle of nowhere on a weekday morning. He flung his jacket over his shoulder, despite it being covered with burs and dust. His clothes: suspenders, trousers and a shirt with sleeves rolled up to the elbow, looked like they might have been more suited for church than tramping through the wild plains, but they were stained and sweaty enough now to look comfortable with the outdoors. Wild rye clung to the cuffs of his pants, his socks and bootstraps. A week's worth of stubble speckled his jaw.

He could see for miles in every direction, another thing he hadn't done for thirteen years, as it can't be done in a tunnel, with only a headlamp revealing a distance of but a few feet. Even outside the mines, in

the sun, the air was gray with coal dust, making visibility as good as that of any foggy morning. Now, crystallized sweat sparkled on his browning skin, clear of the black streaks of grime, and he breathed in the clean, rich smell of soil. The mesmerizing hum of cicadas and katydids, and the trill of the meadowlark made the bells and blaring horns of the mine a distant memory. A brown and orange pattern fluttered on his shoulder. He gently lifted the brush-footed butterfly. A white patch decorated the leading edge of the forewing and two eyespots stood out on the hind wing: an American lady; yes, he still remembered it all.

How he'd come to be back in nature was the simplest thing in the world, he'd been let go. When he'd arrived at the trailer/office a week ago, Harris, the boss, was already there, leaning against his desk. Heinrich checked his watch; on time as ever, but Harris had smiled, his eyebrows coming together with a sympathetic look. The look was meant to comfort, but it always did the opposite because it meant something was wrong. Thirteen years ago, Heinrich had first seen that smile. Harris had been telling a desperate crowd about the tragic cave-in at mine tunnel number eight and how an attempt to rescue the trapped miners might collapse the tunnel. That had been the scariest day of Heinrich's life, and it had turned into the saddest.

But on this morning, a week ago, Harris was talking about 'redundancy' redundantly. Heinrich understood, work at the mine had never been his thing. In fact, he'd kind of expected to be let go from his first day on the job and every day following. He looked down and wondered how often Harris polished his boots and nodded. He was sure Harris was still smiling that pathetic smile but didn't check. When Harris stopped talking, Heinrich simply set down his father's tattered briefcase that he'd inherited the day the mine caved in, muttered "Thank you," and walked out the door. He'd been walking for seven days since.

Thank you? If he had thrown the briefcase right at Harris's face, then Harris might have shown some real concern, he thought. A dragonfly buzzed his shoulder bringing him out of his reminiscing and he realized it all didn't matter now. Harris was probably right anyway, Heinrich hadn't been great at his job. He pushed his sleeves up and sighed. *At least out here,* he mused, *there's no one to please for miles, and that means no one to let down. You can't lose if you don't have to win, right?*

The first day of hiking had surprised him by how far he'd made it from both the mines and his one-steeple town. He'd left the houses and general store behind, and crossed the one bridge, over the two boxcars rusting on their abandoned tracks. Then he'd passed the hay fields, cattle, and barns, many of which were toppled by termites and overgrown by honeysuckle vines. From there on out, no signs of civilization, only plains, distant hills, small streams, eroded banks, wildflowers, and the occasional lonely tree. On the fourth day, he'd arrived at the hills and spotted the first camp: some crude shelters and the shell of a model T resting in the shade of cottonwood trees. He wasn't looking to bother anyone so he'd passed on by it and two more similar camps since.

Today, though, seeing the shelters beneath the oaks, and considering he hadn't spoken to anyone for a week, he decided to explore. He trudged, half slipped down a short slope and approached the grove.

Brushing aside a pale curtain of Spanish moss, he entered the camp. A good number of men stood around in the shade of the trees and several leveled a curious glance his way. The closest fellow, a man in a dirty undershirt and patched trousers, sat on a rock covered with yellow lichen. Heinrich held out his hand.

"Hello," he said. The man's nose was pitted and red as a strawberry. "I'm Heinrich."

The man stuck out his lower lip and his eyebrows popped up.

"Are you now?" he uttered.

Heinrich sheepishly drew back his hand and put it in his pocket and said, "I'm passing through."

The man nodded, apparently plenty of people passed through.

"Can I stay here?"

The man shrugged his shoulders. It wasn't the warmest welcome, but what did Heinrich expect? This man didn't know who he was, (not that a warm welcome would have been given if he did) and in any case, Heinrich preferred to be left alone. The other men in camp had returned to minding their own business, which appeared to amount to blowing the wind around.

"Okay, thanks," Heinrich said. He slid his jacket off his shoulder and stepped past the rock dweller. He turned back and asked, "Can I just set down anywhere?"

The man spat a seed on the ground and stayed as apathetic as before. Heinrich shrugged and continued into the camp, passing the oaks to where less dense alder trees let in more light. A fire pit lay in the center of a dusty common area, surrounded by several men lounging on stumps and logs. Wisps of smoke trailed from their mouths and the heavy fragrance of cigars permeated the air. The men flung their hands about as if in some serious debate, though what could be so important to some wayward vagabonds, Heinrich couldn't guess. Thirty feet from the group, a stream rippled, gleaming where sunbeams poked through the canopy. At a bend in the stream, a dam made of stacked rocks caught debris and stopped up a clear pool large enough to bathe in, though it was doubtful if any of the men took advantage of it. A flimsy-looking footbridge of loose planks lay across the top of the dam. On the other side of the stream, lean-tos of scrap, tin metal and old boards slumped against the trunks of the trees. Behind the lean-tos, further in the shade, little shelters made from squalid canvas hung over lines, protected ragged bedding. Rusty cans, jugs, and broken barrels lay littered and half buried in the dirt around the shelters. Stiff shirts hung forgotten on lines strung up willy-nilly, so it seemed a person would have to walk under or around dangling mildew to get anywhere. Railway ties, rusting machinery, and tires lay discarded in bushes. Corroding wash tubs, rotting crates, and soggy newspapers decomposed with the leaves. *Clearly, one man's trash is another man's treasure . . . then trash again*, Heinrich thought.

He crossed the footbridge and headed past the shelters. Behind a large oak, he found some canvas rotting in the dirt, and using some broken branches, propped it up like a tent and sat down underneath. *I could fit in here eventually*, he thought. *No one will really notice me at all.* For, in general, he kept to himself. He laid back, relieved to be off his feet and left alone, though he realized he was glad to have people nearby. Thinking about them took his mind off thinking about himself.

Though he'd never ventured this far into this country before, he knew of the many types of men that lived here: rascals, wanderers, vagabonds, ramblers, tramps, vagrants, and drifters. He knew that, in the end, they were like him, and really all the same: men who needed to get away. Perhaps they'd had trouble fitting into society or had never found an object or an aim in life. Some may have fit in for a while, but had lost in work or love. Some may have rejected society, preferring less civilized behavior, and some may have been rejected by a society that preferred behavior more civilized. He came to discover that a fair share of the men were veterans, with righteous plenty to get away from, and yet others could offer no notable complaint with life, but were unsatisfied and disillusioned nonetheless. As a whole, the men embodied a thick and varied collection of dreams unrealized or dead, but for them that wasn't such a bad thing. It meant they could give up.

A tall hobo walked into camp at sunset of the same day. A grimy coat hung from his sturdy shoulders and his long stained fingers protruded from fingerless gloves. A thick beard streaked with gray, and parted in the middle so that it pointed in two directions, covered the lower half of his face. A broad-brimmed hat obscured the top. The hobo looked at the men who had gathered around a nursling fire in the fire pit and looked each in the eye as he passed; the men nodded back. Without speaking a word, the hobo strolled straight to a patch of grass, lay down, pulled his hat over his eyes, and brought his hands together on his chest. The other men looked away, allowing the traveler time to relax, but the hobo did not go to sleep. More men gathered around the fire pit. In the darkening shadows, under the cover of his hat, the hobo peeked at the men. His eyes darted from tramp to vagrant, around the fire pit until they rested on one man with suspenders and fine trousers who leaned against a tree behind the circle of men. The hobo closed his eyes.

In the week that followed, the hobo watched this man, but he never approached him. He hid behind trees and watched the man wake up late in the mornings. He crouched in bushes and watched the man sit by the stream and upturn rocks and logs for hours, inspecting the insects and wildlife. At night, sitting in the shadows of other men around the fire, the hobo watched the man accept half eaten cans of food tossed his way. On the seventh day of spying, the hobo was holding still, balanced on a tree branch, and looking from the corners of his eyes as his man inspected a wasp nest in the hollow of the next tree. Both dodged the buzzing insects shooting to and fro. Neither man saw the fat man approach.

"I knew I recognized that face, Patrick's son, no doubt, no doubt," the fat man said. Broken capillaries spread like spider webs on his pudgy cheeks, parted in a senseless smile.

Heinrich turned around startled. The hobo held his breath.

"What are you doing way out here?" the fat man asked.

"Not much." Heinrich made a long step away from the wasp nest. "Quit working there... the mine, two weeks ago."

A wasp landed on Heinrich's shoulder.

III The Camp

"Watch out." The fat man said in a hushed tone and took an ungain-ly step forward with a heavy hand raised. Heinrich, noticing the wasp, leaned away.

"That's okay," he said. "I got it. You could get stung swatting like that, plus the other wasps wouldn't be too happy about it." Heinrich jerk-ed the fabric of his shirt, catapulting the wasp off. The fat man shrugged.

"Quit huh, good for you. They canned me over a decade ago. Can't imagine why?" he smiled drunkenly, his voice had gotten loud. Then he frowned and quieted down. "Sorry about your old man, a terrible shame. But say, that still don't explain what you're doin' out here? He wouldn't want you homeless with the likes of me."

Heinrich ducked under another zipping wasp.

"Well, I guess he'll never know. There's a lot he'll never know, and that's for the better as far as I'm concerned."

Heinrich turned abruptly and walked away, forgetting his jacket in the dirt. The fat man shrugged and headed back to camp. When he was sure the area was vacated, the hobo climbed down from the tree and picked up Heinrich's jacket.

The logs and stumps encircling the fire pit accommodated thirty men, leaving a few others to rest in the dirt. Nighttime rarely brought a chill, so none felt the need to huddle closer to the heat. In the gray dusk, a flicker escaped the teepee of dry branches built on the ash of the morn-ing's fire. The men opened dinted cans to discover the meal for the night and placed them around the fire. Two fellows who had actually exerted some effort during the day arranged three trout on skewers above the flickering flames.

When the fire became the only source of light, before the stars be-gan to twinkle, the teepee of branches toppled in a huff of tiny bright embers. The fire's red-orange glow found greasy fingers, contented fac-es, and glistening beards going up and down. Cans lay littered around the men's feet. All was quiet but for the whine of steaming sap that always preceded a sharp pop and slight puff of ash. The first cricket chirped, signaling the nightly serenade's approach, then a second sounded from deeper in the trees.

"Six dead bodies bleeding in the moonlight. Haunts me still," blurted a gaunt man, interrupting everyone's thoughts, or lack thereof. His hunched back, and the crutch in the dirt next to him suggested he was a veteran. His right leg ending before it reached the ground and his choice of conversation all but confirmed it. He scowled, showing the expression that had folded the ever-present lines on his face, then opened his mouth again as if to say more.

"That's enough Earl," warned a man whose belly had clearly found no objection to the meal of canned food surprise, but whose expression showed he'd found objection to what the gaunt man was saying. Earl shut his mouth. That being settled, and the men finishing their meals, a murmur of general conversation began to hum as more empty cans and fish bones were tossed on the ground.

Heinrich stared into a can of watery green beans. The men had discussed the war every night he'd been there, which was a stark contrast to when he was a boy, when the war was actually happening. His father wouldn't let it be mentioned around the house. "That's nothing for you to worry about Heinrich," he'd say. But it had worried him, and despite his father's attempts to shelter him from the war, he'd heard about it from the other kids in the neighborhood when they'd come to help him raise his blue-belly lizards. He'd shown the kids how to hunt flies and spiders to feed the lizards and received nightmares from their stories of men who would never come home.

"No... it's not enough, Sam. Someone should speak of him!" Earl blurted again and louder, snapping Heinrich back to the present. He looked up from his beans. The conversations around him had stopped. Earl leered around at the circle of fire lit faces. The men on either side of him leaned away.

Sam, the man who had quieted Earl the first time, folded his arms over a heavy belly and sighed.

"Out with it then, Earl. What are you talking about?" He looked at the other men and nodded, and they all stayed quiet. With a ready audience, Earl hesitated a moment as though gathering his courage, then whispered,

"No one knows the truth of it."

Now, every man leaned in. Those who were not veterans leaned in a little further. Earl shuddered, looked at the ground, and began his haunting tale.

"It happened on a reconnaissance mission. We were scouting a long ways out and late one afternoon we ambushed a squad of six gray coats. We'd found them at the base of the Silverado range and I don't think they'd expected anyone out so far because they were making an early supper and hadn't their weapons near them. We simply walked out of the trees, rifles leveled, and ordered for hands up. It was me who, one by

one, took down their arms and bound their wrists.

"We hadn't expected to take any prisoners, being only four in our party, but I guess we just couldn't resist when we found them unawares. Sure enough though, the custody of six of the enemy proved a difficult problem. We checked our rations and checked the map and realized what we already knew: we didn't have enough to feed our prisoners and were too far from anywhere we could take them. Advancing in the field while guarding prisoners would be impossible and, at the same time, so would maintaining a secure position. We decided we should split up, though it would be more dangerous for each group, in order for one to return the prisoners and the other to keep advancing. Discussions on how to split our party became heated, and as night crept in without our having reached a resolution, we agreed to sleep on it.

"The prisoners were hogtied and bound together at the base of a tree. I gathered straws to determine who would stand the first watch when a man who called himself Frank, a quiet fellow none of us knew too well, volunteered. Theo, the oldest of the squad, drew the short straw and joined Frank, as myself and Clarence prepared to rest.

"I knew something was wrong when I opened my eyes in the middle of the night and had the most awful feeling I've ever felt. I was trying to figure what had waked me when two shots cracked about thirty yards away. I grabbed my rifle from underneath my pack and scrambled toward the tree when I heard what sounded like someone gagging. I reached the tree and was relieved to see, with the light of a dull moon, the captives still bound there. They looked like they were sleeping with their heads resting on their chests. But then I saw a sheen from a dark stain spreading down one man's shirt. I heard the gagging sound again. Old Theo was kneeling in the dirt and retching into the bushes. Then I saw Frank, just standing there holding his rifle with smoke swirling from the barrel like ghosts."

Earl closed his eyes before continuing.

"How could we have known he'd do that?" he wailed. He pressed his chin hard into his chest. "Next thing I knew, Frank was gone, vanished like a spirit..." He took a long pull from an earthen jug.

"We didn't go after him. We didn't even speak about it. Without prisoners to worry about, we kept going as if it was all okay. We were cowards!" The firelight danced in his glistening eyes.

The circle of men stared at Earl with mouths agape. A few men, frightened by the story, glanced over their shoulders into the black of the forest. The veterans, which were most of the older fellows, exchanged sheepish looks with each other. One of them who had a long, stained, white beard removed his crumpled hat and drawled in a gravelly voice,

"The vengeance of the Executioner is what you witnessed. Be thankful if you never saw him in battle." He stroked his beard with a hand that was missing two fingers. "No mercy," he continued. "Yours is one of many squads he joined and if ever prisoners were taken, they'd be dead by morning. That was his way. Whatever name he went by, it's him, the Executioner! Sorry truth of it all is, at the beginning, we thought he was doing us all a favor. I mean, less of the enemy right? Those were hard times."

"Possessed by a demon or one himself I say," uttered another veteran in overalls. "And he vanished like one too. You know, in the end, when we did finally go after him, to make him pay for his crimes, regardless of whose side he was on, he was never found."

"Then may he rot in hell!" said a short man from under a heavy mustache.

"Back to from where he came," said another.

"If only I had shot him then," Earl lamented.

"Well, if he is out there still and I ever find him, I'll skin him alive," said a young fellow who tottered and spilled his drink.

"Only after I toss him into a nest of rattlesnakes first," said another.

The entire company of men, civilian and veteran alike, nodded in agreement and continued to suggest punishments they might inflict on the Executioner, like in some contest of cruelty, with each suggestion of vengeance or justice more vicious than the last. Only two men, perhaps on account of being the newest to camp, did not join in the contest:

Heinrich and the hobo. They only listened. After the imaginations of the men started to stumble and the conversation died down, the hobo leaned in from the shadows. All eyes turned toward him as he was the only one standing, and the men quieted completely. Only the sound of the fire crackling could be heard. Heinrich was especially curious because he had never seen the hobo before, despite the fact that the hobo had been watching him for a week. He would have noticed a tall man whose beard pointed in two directions. The hobo's eyes flashed in the shadow of his broad hat. For the first time since entering the camp, the hobo spoke. He said in a firm and resonating voice,

> *"You who would have this evil man ended in evil ways,*
> *Ask, how should you be treated if you should go astray?*
>
> *Who do you suggest should handle these executions?*
> *Could you so easily deliver such morbid retributions?*
> *Is that the way you presume to show your might,*
> *To do as evil does, and somehow make things right?*
>
> *Would you become crooked to correct a crooked man?*
> *Would you react in kind, then boast of blood stained hands?*
> *What sort of twisted justice do you hope to gain,*
> *If attained using this same wicked, senseless pain?*
>
> *Yours are weakened thoughts, threatening and frightened,*
> *Do not fight your fears, they are a chance to be enlightened!*
> *Let terror not inspire terror, let understanding be explored,*
> *Stop this hope for a life to end. Hope for a life to be restored!"*

The fire shrank back, cowering just above the smoldering coals. The men fidgeted in their seats. Only a few had enough nerve to look at the strange hobo who was looking intensely straight into the fire. Suddenly, a strong wind rushed into the camp, blowing through the hobo's coat and stoking the fire into a blaze that flared up six feet high. The men reared back from the conflagration with a yelp. Branches snapped in the howling trees and leaves whipped past the faces of the assembly as they covered their eyes from the dust that had been blown into the air. Then, just as quickly, the swirling leaves settled and fire dropped back down to the coals. The startled men looked at each other, brushed dirt from their beards and sat back down. Not a word was spoken for a spell and they just stared at the fire. Eventually, they found their drinks, and after a few sips, small conversations started up again. However, none of them mentioned the Executioner again, and the hobo, who'd been the center of attention but a moment before, went unnoticed in the shadows once more.

Heinrich finally released his grip on a blanket he'd brought up as a shield from the blaze. *Has everyone completely forgotten what just happened?* he asked himself, thoroughly confused. He looked at the strange hobo again. Across the circle of men, the hobo's pupils appeared as two black voids in two burning suns. They focused on Heinrich like they would swallow him in. Fireflies flickered around the hobo's head, casting weird illuminations on his beard parted in two. Heinrich looked away and then looked back. The hobo still stared, holding still as a statue; the voids of his eyes beckoned. Heinrich looked away again. *What the devil?* He checked one last time. The hobo was gone.

Beneath his moldy shelter, Heinrich readjusted the blanket he'd found by the fire and rolled over yet again. Several incidents from the evening disturbed him. He had no idea what he would do if he met the Executioner. Maybe he'd just say 'thank you' like he'd said to Harris, and let the Executioner put him out of his misery. No, he'd probably just run like hell. The hobo's weird speech and stranger stare also worried him. *I'm out of here first thing in the morning,* he vowed and rolled over again.

As he closed his eyes a vision of warm blood spreading out in a cold night crept like a shadow at the back of his mind. He tried to keep it from taking over his thoughts, but his efforts dwindled like a flame with no candle left to burn. The candlelight of his thoughts went out and the world became as black as the Hobo's eyes. A vision of men unable to escape from a soundless mine surged forward and a wave of nausea overcame him. He shuddered and gripped his blanket tighter. The chirping crickets would not stop. The moon hinted behind the hills but refused to show itself. He closed his eyes again. *Life is cruel,* he thought.

Chapter II
The Whistle

Early the next morning, Heinrich rubbed the sleep from his eyes. A light mist crept through the silent trees. The fluttering calls of the prairie warblers hadn't yet begun. He would get away before anyone woke up. He quietly got to his feet, brushed the dirt from his pants, and made his way to the fire pit, avoiding stepping on any twigs. He blew away the white ash that weightlessly covered still hot coals and piled on a handful of tinder. Once smoke started rising, he picked up a blackened pot and headed to the stream. Off to his right, he heard the crackle of dry oak leaves and he looked to see who else was up. Ten yards away, he spotted a faint depression in the earth where the grass lay flattened. The hobo's hat lay at the top of the depression. Heinrich dropped the pot with a bang. He scrambled and grabbed it up again, cursing under his breath. The hobo had probably just left in the night and forgotten his hat; one never did know who would be gone or arrived on any given day.

Heinrich filled the pot at the stream and surveyed the sleeping camp as he returned to the fire. *One cup of coffee and I'm gone,* he decided. He fed a larger stick into the nest of hungry young flames pecking greedily at the sky. As the smoke rose it flashed brilliant white, revealing rays of morning sun piercing the trees. He missed the early morning. A large movement rustled to his right breaking his reverie. To his dismay, the hobo sat down two stumps away and held grimy, fingerless-gloved hands towards the fire. The only other thing disrupting the morning was the even snores of the others, sounding like a team of lumberjacks sawing away at the trees, which meant Heinrich was on his own with the hobo.

He leaned forward to tend the fire hoping to feign enough concentration to discourage interruption, but it did not work.

"Do you hear that sound?" the hobo asked.

Heinrich poked the fire casually, trying to hide how startled he was, and looked up. The hobo stared at him just as he had the night before, searching, maybe sizing him up, as he squinted and bobbed his head ever so slightly. His stare switched from one of Heinrich's eyes to the other. *Does he really hear something?* Heinrich wondered, for he heard nothing but snores, the crackle of the small fire, and a quail cooing in the distance. Heinrich shook his head indicating he heard nothing out of the ordinary. The hobo nodded encouragingly, so Heinrich listened again. Nothing. The fire needed more fuel. He itched his leg. Then something blared far away, and blared again.

"What was that?" Heinrich whispered with surprise. "Where's it coming from?"

The hobo answered,

"It's just a whistle on the wind, but this time, it blows sooo strange,
I hear the click, I hear the clack, it brings me back. It's the train...
But it does not come for me, I've done my time. Your time to go!
Heed me boy, for I know things, things that you have yet to know!

The ways outside are boundless, it is hard to know your plan,
If you hear a call and you are able, do all you can . . . do all you can!"

The hobo had stepped over and clutched Heinrich's arm. The two
men searched each other's eyes. The hobo released his grip, apologetic
for getting so worked up, and sat back on the stump. Questions erupted
in Heinrich's head. There weren't any train tracks nearby. *Where could a*
train whistle come from? How did this man hear that whistle so long before me?

He considered asking the hobo more about the whistle, but the
man seemed unstable and made Heinrich wary. Also, when the hobo
had grabbed him, Heinrich had seen leaves, twigs, and dirt in his beard;
graying hair stuck together like a tangle of cobwebs; and a landscape of
various molds covering his coat. The smell of any of these aspects, but
especially united as one, struck like a fist on the nose. He decided he'd
rather remove himself from the hobo's company and learn about the
whistle on his own. He'd planned to leave that morning anyhow.

"I'm going to check it out," he said, standing and backing away.

The hobo only nodded and then held out a tightly packed bundle.
Heinrich paused, then recognizing the bundle as his own jacket, grabbed
it like a mouse gingerly snatching a crumb. *How could I have forgotten*
this? He put the jacket on and felt the pocket. Thankfully, the letter was
still there.

"Thank you," he uttered and in quickly turning away, struck a rock
with his foot. He winced but tried to keep his composure as he strode
away with a slight limp. The hobo smiled, sat up straight, rested his
hands on his knees and closed his eyes as if beginning a meditation.

Chapter III
The Train

Heinrich left the camp, following the stream towards its source. After a quarter mile of hiking, the shore narrowed and the banks steepened until he came to a small waterfall. The rocks proved too slippery and steep to climb so he grabbed roots jutting out from the eroded banks, and pulled himself up to the floor of a small wood. A beetle flew right past his nose and landed on the limb of a nearby tree. He walked over to it, excited and careful to not scare the creature because he recognized it as a speckled eastern Hercules beetle. He had only ever seen one in his field guide as a kid. *Why has it taken so long to find you!* he mused just as the whistle sounded again, louder though still far off. He looked up only to look back and find the beetle was gone.

He headed through the wood in the direction of the whistle, thankful that the hobo, strange as he was, prompted him on his way that morning, even if it had been by scaring him. He felt the letter in his jacket again, relieved anew that it was still there and anxious that he had almost forgotten it. *Thank God that dirty hobo returned my jacket!* The letter was from his father, who had included it in his will. Heinrich used to read the letter often and he knew the words by heart. The last line, which had once filled him with promise, read: *"You, my son, are great; you will do great things."* His father had been so optimistic about his future. "The bright light at the end of my tunnel each day," his father would say when arriving home late, blackened with coal dust, "is that you will have a better life than me." *Not yet,* Heinrich thought.

As it had turned out, ironically, after his father had died in that cave-in thirteen years ago, Heinrich had just taken his job. His father had never wanted him to work the mines. In fact, there had been a day, when, not knowing what to do with his life, Heinrich had asked for a position at the mines and his father had said, "Over my dead body." His father couldn't have ever imagined that that is exactly what would happen. *The mine was a secure job*, Heinrich mused, *and good enough for Dad, so why not good enough for me?* It had been years since he had read the whole letter now. After a while it had only reminded him of disappointment and how wrong his father had been about him. He had not done great things.

Heinrich stepped from the woods into the glare of the morning sun which eased him out of his melancholy. Shielding his eyes, he looked at a small valley below where, to his surprise, a train lumbered through golden fields. Heinrich could have sworn he'd hiked through the same valley a week before and there had not been any tracks. He squinted and shook his head.

"How the heck did I miss them?" he whispered.

White smoke puffed from a hefty smokestack painted like the rest of the engine, white with scarlet and gold trimmings. Directly behind the engine trailed a squat coal-car, and a tall, narrow boxcar lurched behind that. The following car was long and lined with bars and, as it turned out, each of the cars following were also uniquely shaped, but all in relatively good shape despite their fading colors. A maroon boxcar caught Heinrich's attention. Its sliding door stood open and a man was leaning out waving. Heinrich squinted again and had the impression that the man was waving at him. He began to hike down the slope through the dead-nettle and violet thistle blossom to get a closer look.

As he neared the approaching train, he felt its heavy rumble in the ground and established that the waving man was indeed waving at him. The man wore dark pressed trousers, a striped vest, and a bowtie. His hair parted down the middle of his head and likewise on his upper lip in the form of a small waxed mustache. As the engine rolled past, chugging and hissing, a wall of warm air smashed into Heinrich and he realized it was going faster than he had thought. The maroon boxcar approached

IV A Train

and the man inside cupped a hand to the side of his mouth and began to yell, but he could not be heard over the whining wheels and clacking couplings. The man sped by and started waving both arms. Heinrich, unsure of what he had missed but sure he had missed something, jogged after the car only to find the train picking up speed. He held his jacket to keep it from flapping behind him and began to dash after the waving man. One car length behind, he heard,

> *"Do not stray too long in these wilds,*
> *Beware the aimless and beguiled!*
> *Fate does not come often to those out in these plains,*
> *This is barren land, grab my hand, get on this train!*
> *We are moving, let's get going, forget this place! Make haste, make haste!*
> *Don't be old and in the way and off the tracks at the end of days."*

The man's waxed hairstyle began fraying in the wind. Heinrich found himself running faster than he could remember ever running. The man called out again,

> *"Come on now, be quick, now's not the time for looking back,*
> *This train is getting faster and we are always losing track.*
> *We won't come this way again, these wheels are really rolling,*
> *Though they don't know where they roll, they go, so let's get going!*
> *You can't always be running to catch up from behind,*
> *Grab ahold and learn that fate can pull the weight sometimes!"*

Hanging out of the train, the man thrust out his hand. When he judged he was running at the pace of the train, Heinrich grabbed for the entreating hand and felt it close like a vise. His feet lurched off the ground and he held on with all his might. He leapt along the oily railway ties rushing at him. Singing steel wheels sliced along rigid rails only a foot away from his ankles. His hat flew away behind him, but he could not bother about it now. The train did not pause, hesitate, or so much

as shudder when he found footing on a low step. The step yanked his
foot and body along with. With a moving train, it is either on or off.
There is no in-between and Heinrich had the sense that he was linked to
something he had not experienced for a very long time, something he'd
lost—something absolute.

The man's grip held true. He hauled Heinrich up the small ladder of the boxcar and went on hollering above the rushing air and
flapping clothes,

> *"Confound it, step there. Have you gone unfit for waiting?*
> *Forget your hat and hang on tight. Stop this hesitating.*
> *Pull yourself up my man, I know this is all brand new,*
> *But have some faith in me at least. Help me helping you!"*

Heinrich steadied himself on the threshold of the doorway. He had
made it. He let out a chuckle of both relief and exhilaration and realized
he was still grasping the man's hand when the man began to shake it.

"The label's Able," the man introduced with a smile and smart nod.

Heinrich, still catching his breath, nodded back and looked around
the interior of the boxcar. Loose straw covered the floorboards. Towards the front, stenciled crates were stacked almost to the ceiling and
secured with netting. Looking to the back of the boxcar, Heinrich's vision adjusted for the shade and he detected a glinting light. In the far
corner, a man stood with shackles on his hands and feet, and from each
shackle dangled a heavy chain that was bolted to the wall. White lines
crisscrossed the man's face like war paint, but were raised, and Heinrich
realized they were lines that would never wash away—scars. The man
looked up. Heinrich yelped and stumbled backward. The wind howled
and yanked at his coat and his back foot dropped out of the train. With
mongoose-like reflexes, Able snagged Heinrich's shirt and pulled him
up to the brink again.

"What's going on?" Heinrich gasped. Able lowered his chin and said,

"You startle easily, one small scare and out you go,
Be curious, not afraid, of the things you do not know.

You might learn something here, don't be so affected,
It may be time you learn to expect the unexpected.
The surprise of a surprise depends on your reaction,
I saved your life because I expect surprise to happen.

I advise you stay onboard; you don't want to miss this ride,
Make yourself at home, set down your things and stay inside.
Now welcome onboard again, we'll be picking up the pace,
I'll introduce you to my friend, but please . . . don't ask about his face."

He patted Heinrich's shoulder and led the way. Heinrich wasn't sure
he wanted any more surprises, but he was not ready to jump from the
speeding train. He followed Able to the corner of the car but stopped a
yard in front of the shackled man. The man smiled, held out a weathered hand and with a thickly accented voice, introduced himself as Ivan.
Eased by the man's mild nature, Heinrich leaned in and shook his deli-

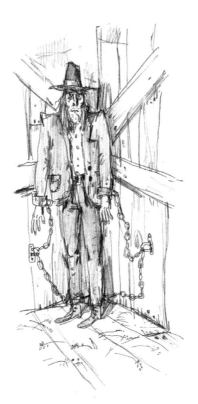

cate hand, but he kept his attention on the chains and locks rather than the man's scarred face.

"Why the chains?" Heinrich asked cautiously. "Are you a wanted man?" Ivan laughed and caressed his jaw. The car jolted causing the chains from his wrist to jangle.

"Yes, in fact, perhaps for the first time I am.
Though not for something desperate, I'm not a wicked man,
I have been hired for a job, but I am prone to recklessness,
Sometimes I stray, and then I find myself irrelevant.
You see, I become distracted even though I've much to gain,
So I've taken some precautions and have locked myself in chains."

Ivan's pale eyes flashed as he gazed past Heinrich at the fields rushing by. With a faraway look, he continued,

"I've tried to hide my poor face, so scarred it made me blush,
I said the scars don't define me, because I did not know what does.

But traveler, beware the pains or the shackles you refuse.
If you try to reject them all, you'll be forever on the move.
Like the men who are never satisfied, who feel life is hard and curse their fate,
And who take to the roads and the highways, always striving to escape.

They run from the known, from being known. They run from knowing,
Until they have nowhere to go and no reason to stop their going.
For they reject too much, but I don't wish to be forever bound,
To be defined by what I'm not. No, lock me up till I am found!"

Ivan had become a little excited. Spittle leaked from his scarred mouth as he continued to stare out at the hills. *You are a brave and optimistic man,* Heinrich thought. Able had sat down on a crate and was leaning against the jostling wall of the car, listening calmly. Heinrich followed suit, pulled over a crate and sat down.

He wasn't sure Ivan's warnings about running away from things applied to him. Sure, he'd left town and everything behind two weeks prior, more certain he was not a miner than who he actually was, but before that he'd more or less shackled himself to a job for thirteen years. After his father had passed, and not having a better plan of what to do with his life, it had seemed the most secure thing to do. In thirteen years he'd still never found a better plan. *Unless,* he thought, *was I running from finding one the whole time?*

He glanced at the open door and watching the mustard flowers whizz by in a blur, he let his thoughts blow away with the wind. Ivan sat down with them and Heinrich was about to ask Able why he'd been waving for him to get on the train when Able smiled, pulled a deck of cards from his vest pocket, and began to deal a game. Heinrich leaned forward, stretching his back, and watched Able dexterously twirl their fates into three piles. Instinctively, Heinrich gathered his cards and began to arrange and assess his fortune. He'd never been great at card games though he knew how to play. Able squared his own hand without so much as looking what he had, then he spoke, answering a few of the questions Heinrich had been about to ask, but with the most unexpected answers, creating even more questions,

> *"Heinrich, bid a farewell to these wild plains,*
> *You've just hopped aboard a wild circus train.*
>
> *We head to our final stop, a very unusual show,*
> *Lead by a remarkable man we call the Great Mephisto.*
> *You will see amazing things, many you will doubt are true,*
> *So take heed, what you discover there will be entirely up to you.*
>
> *To pass the time: Mephisto's story, and how it came to be,*
> *He was found and loved by a mermaid when lost way out to sea."*

Chapter IV
The Great Mephisto

Heinrich looked up immediately. He held a card frozen in midair and focused on Able as his mind tried to process what it had just heard. *Mermaid?* But Able didn't seem to be joking. He didn't even look up before he continued right along, telling his tale, summarized as follows.

***

One cold, gray morning, a stumbling fisherman, who was sobering to the fact that he'd been up all night not sober, discovered a babe wrapped in a woolen blanket and lying on the shore, inches away from a lapping tide. He rescued the bundle and quickly realized he had no idea what to do with it, in fact, he had never held a babe before, so he brought it to the nearest town and roused the doctor. The doctor readily determined that no local in his small town was responsible for the child, as none were due, and, sadly, that no family had the capacity to become so. After assuring the poor sailor that his discovery would be provided for, the doctor sent him on his way and entrusted the care of the child to the local orphanage. Anything about the babe before that point, including where and to whom he was born, would ever remain as obscure and mysterious as the misty morning on which he was found.

The local orphanage operated on the generosity of three elderly ladies: two sisters who had never let a man get between them, and a widow who had miscarried when her husband was lost at sea, and vowed to forever care for abandoned souls, as she found herself to be. The ladies did

the best they could with limited resources and space but had had to turn down new arrivals for years due to capacity. However, when the doctor arrived with a newborn—only hours old—and his story, the ladies could not overcome their curiosity about, or their sympathies for, such a help-less babe. The sisters thanked heaven for delivering the child from the vile hands of the drunk man that found him, and the widow believed that if they took the babe in, the babe would really only have been abandoned for but a few hours of his life, and it would be her swiftest rescue.

They provided for the babe by each doing with a little less, which they were used to anyway, and which is often easier for those that have little as they've learned what really matters in this world, and which turned out to be a small price to pay for the joys they received. A complete wardrobe for the babe was tailored from a curtain, whose room had always needed a little more light. As for the added burden of his care, the other orphans took delight in playing and caring for the babe, making the whole lot of them easier to manage.

The babe, of course, had no name, but one was understood to have been given to him by a three-year-old girl who cared for him like he was her baby brother. Overhearing the matrons often say the word 'mystery' when referring to the babe, the little girl began to call him, with her burgeoning grasp on speech, 'my mysto,' which sounded more like 'mymeesto.' The matrons, hearing this, and deciding it easiest to call the babe whatever the orphans called him, adopted what they thought the girl was saying, also thinking it had a certain ring to it: "Mephisto."

Now, the question of one's origins is an early one for an abandoned child and the matrons always answered it as soon as it came up, clearly and with the truth, in order to avoid rumors amongst the children. So, at a very young age, Mephisto learned of the inauspicious location where he'd been found and that he'd been left there. Rita, the widow whose husband had never returned from sea, had been the one to tell him, remarking as she did so, "'Tis such a shame, 'tis such a cruel shame for a sweet boy like you." However, Mephisto didn't consider his situation a shame at all; he considered it providential that he'd been discovered and given shelter when he'd been at his most vulnerable. Furthermore, he considered his unique introduction to the world as an indication that fate had a different plan for him and that his life was destined to be special.

In the small town surrounding the orphanage, little ever happened, but to its harbor, sailors would arrive with stories of everything that does happen and an undercurrent of intrigue ever lurked through the streets like the low morning mist. Strange stories of adventure and the unknown spread and grew unchecked as few citizens had experience or desire enough to refute them. Growing up, Mephisto and the other abandoned children reveled in telling and embellishing on the gossip they heard of the outside world, without any consideration of what was real or what real was. By the age of ten, however, Mephisto yearned to test the truth of the stories against the proof of experience, hoping, of course, that the results would be a match. Only one week after his tenth birthday, he decided to cast his fate into the wind, as he had been cast by his parents, and see what fate, given another chance, might do. On a cold, gray morning, with a coat made from a curtain, Mephisto left the orphanage.

***

Man, *this fellow can talk!* thought Heinrich. Sweat beaded on the back of his neck despite the cool air blowing through the boxcar door. Able had thoroughly captivated him with his story, and to be so captivated by a speaker is a rare joy. All the while, however, Heinrich had also maintained a certain focus on the games at hand and won quite a few rounds. Ivan, by comparison, had not won a single game. He leaned back in his corner with his chains and looked relaxed, smiling even.

"Wait," Heinrich interjected, "A ten-year-old left the only home he'd ever known? A kid just took his fate into his own hands?"

Able nodded and replied,

> *"Who's to say one's not fated to decide as one decides?*
> *To make certain choices, no matter what fortunes coincide?*
> *Some folks look to the sky and patiently wait for signs,*
> *But what if they looked inside and found their own designs?"*

"Well, if he was designed to be that adventurous, I'm impressed," Heinrich said. "Though, maybe he was just naive about the harsher realities of life." He cocked his head and gave Able a knowing look. Able didn't seem to notice the look and replied,

> *"Some men think life is rough and struggle with a harsh existence,*
> *But when free to choose their fate, they show a furious resistance.*
> *Because struggles define their value, but really they heft the easy load,*

Find out who you are, define your own value. That's the harder road."

Could that be true? Heinrich thought. *Was working at the mine just me hefting the easy load?* He brushed away the idea and looked down at his cards. All low, nothing good. He'd likely fold. *Well,* he thought, *what do you do if you aren't dealt anything good?* Able, as though reading his thoughts, indicated Ivan with a wave of his hand and said in a lighter tone,

> *"Look at Ivan's easy smile even though he's not winnin',*
> *Maybe the game is not determined by the cards you're given.*
> *If you lose or win, or the tactics you've employed,*
> *Maybe it's determined by whether it was enjoyed."*

Able looked at his cards and with a look of surprise lay down a three of a kind and a pair of aces. Heinrich folded, tossing his cards down, but Ivan slowly lowered his cards face up on the floor. It was then that Able smiled deeply. Ivan's first win was with a perfect hand. Heinrich was utterly amazed, he'd never seen a perfect hand happen in a game before. With a chuckle, Able gathered the cards and continued his story of the Great Mephisto.

***

Whether Mephisto was designed with wanderlust in his blood, or it came from his parents, who'd proved it ran rampant through their veins when they left a child by the sea, or it developed in him on the morning he spent as a babe, alone beneath the stars, or it came from the stories he'd heard from the sailors and other children; his decision to leave at such a young age was fateful. He left a note for the matrons of the orphanage which read:

> *"You gave me grace, I could want for little more.*

Yet I cannot ignore a yearning to explore.
Know I will be well and always will be faithful,
That life is good, and that I'll be forever grateful,
And no matter what happens, no matter my position,
I will look after the abandoned, and give as you have given."

He walked through the morning fog, directly to the docks where the stories he'd heard originated, and where he reckoned the more opportunities to find his fate awaited. The docks were alive with shouts of men preparing for sea and the action of equipment being both unloaded and hoisted aboard various ships. He snuck through the throng of wool coated sailors while keeping a low profile under the marine mist. As he trotted along the tar covered planks of the pier, he kept a look out for anything inspiring while also avoiding musty nets, barrels of fish, and scurrying crabs. Seagulls crowded the sky and pelicans perched on pilings, which they had stained white and given an acrid smell. The birds eyed the fishing vessels weaving in the foamy dark water amongst the tall ships. Looking up, Mephisto marveled at sailors securing sails ninety feet in the air and wondered how they kept track of all those lines. Beneath the bow of a towering ship, a light, colored shape caught both a ray of dawn and his eye. A fair maiden with red braided hair and her lower half designed as a fish tail, stared out to the horizon.

Though her wood was sodden and cracked, and the paint was peeling, Mephisto stood enchanted; he did not even flinch when a brown rat scurried over his foot. She was nothing like he had imagined. In the orphanage, he'd heard a story of mermaids who snatched sailors from their beds and it had given him nightmares and the impression that mermaids were evil. The sisters had comforted him with the explanation that mermaids were just the fancy of men with mead-muddled minds, but now, seeing the craftsmanship of this statue, Mephisto wondered if both he and the kindly women might be wrong. The figurehead was beautiful, not frightening at all, and whoever had carved her with such detail must have both been quite sober and, he figured, seen a mermaid in the flesh.

Despite the cursing sailors surrounding the vessel, and its imposing height, Mephisto made straight for the gangway, grabbed the handrail and began stepping up the planks. When he was halfway up, a man covered with tattoos and hair appeared at the top and began to bounce down with a crate and belly too large to see beneath. Mephisto gripped the handrail and swung out over the murky water sloshing between the ship and the pier, but as the man approached, the smell of sour eggs struck so powerfully that Mephisto tried to plug his nose and in letting go with one hand, he lost his grip. He grasped onto the planks and held on for dear life as the man bounded past, coming within inches of crushing his fingers. On an upward bounce of the gangway, Mephisto swung himself onto it again and gained the deck.

The crew, busy hoisting crates from the holds and securing sails, barely noticed Mephisto, but them that did, glared at him with a look that warned he keep to himself, though they need not have worried. Their rough appearances alone had Mephisto uncertain that coming aboard had been the right idea. Each man wore at least a dagger or a pistol under his belt, many had both. Mephisto sidestepped to the bulwarks while trying to spot anyone among the crew that looked decent enough to approach. The smell of urine and rot wafted up from the holds. A shadow crept over him and to his left the deck boards creaked, but he was too afraid to see what caused it. A seagull suddenly screeched, making him jump back and look up. A man in a black, long coat loomed above him and blocked the sun. Mephisto quailed. The man spoke with a hiss,

"Welcome aboard lad, let me guess, the maid caught your attention,
You saw her on the bow and she has filled your heart with questions.
I am Captain Rabar, her tale, more wild than you could imagine.
It happens a craftsman fashioned her, while overcome with passion.

Follow me, my boy, to my cabin down below,
I shall tell you all her secrets, all that you wish to know."

V The Docks

Some things are better left unknown, but sadly youth has not learned to know that yet. Mephisto, amazed that the captain knew the mermaid had led him aboard, followed the captain up a short set of steep stairs to the quarterdeck and into the shadows of a doorway. In a dark passageway, loose floorboards, something dripping from overhead, and musty air induced in Mephisto a dark feeling far different than the hope the mermaid had inspired on the pier. When Mephisto could barely see a thing at all, Captain Rabar opened a heavy door revealing his quarters, and Mephisto's impressions abruptly changed again. In a cabin decorated with ornately carved wood, a hoard of treasure was collected. Shining plates and goblets of precious metal lay heaped on a mess of tapestries and silk. Coins and jewels lay scattered amongst bowls and chests, all of it tangled in strings of pearls as though it had been violently jostled together in a storm. Mephisto gaped at the reckless heaps of riches, curious that they were covered with dust and cobwebs, and did not notice Rabar close and lock the door. Suddenly, the captain clapped his hands right behind Mephisto's head and snarled,

> *"You nasty little ingrate, turn and look upon my face!*
> *See foul filth pour from my mouth as I spit black teeth about the place.*
> *Know me for your fate, so that you shall ever grieve,*
> *Know this for your prison, from which you shall never leave!"*

Mephisto reeled back. As Rabar grinned, rotting teeth did indeed fall from his mouth and though he spat them out, there were always more. Rabar chuckled and continued,

> *"Poor fool, you're not the first to come asking 'bout the maid,*
> *Other seekers sought her secrets, but a price is to be paid.*
> *You who seek a fresh horizon, who want the strange and new,*
> *Find that life is pain and drudgery as one amongst my crew.*

Before you feel rudely tricked, allow that I explain,
The man that made that mermaid went utterly insane.
And I am doing you a favor, for destiny is just delusion!
Any that trust in fate and seek, find discontent and ruin."

Rabar gestured with a hand tipped by black fingernails to the heaps
of riches in his cabin.

"The foolish think themselves precious, as though divinely graced,
They think they deserve it all, but their lusts will end in rot and waste.
In life, you too will fail, cause misery, age, and die, and turn to dust,
But here you will avoid all that; you'll never ruin love or break a trust.

Here you'll avoid man's folly, you'll not become the source of all your pain,
You'll not know the loss of failed hopes or the burn of greed inside your veins.
No need to fear what you might become, or to know your terrible nature,
Here you may keep your pride at bay with constant, mindless labor!"

And here Rabar trembled with a mighty fury,

"So curse you, not I! You are the fool who allows himself deceived.
Know that fate is cruel and man is worse, nothing is as you believed.
Better that you stayed home. What made you think that you were special?
If you knew a thing of life at all, you'd wish that yours was uneventful!"

Rabar panted and looked at his own shaking hands. Mephisto shrunk backward and tried to put a tall chair between himself and the captain. Rabar grabbed the chair, flung it to the ground and roared,

"That figurehead is a deception, a beautiful lie beneath the spar,
Just like the ways of man; we hide how terrible we truly are!

Why would you be different? We were born and life is pain,
Kill your aspirations, failure is your most certain gain.
Remember this, when your back is breaking on this ship of filth and tar,
*Better you toil than know yourself. **Be ashamed of who you are!"***

***

Able looked up from his narration to see how his audience was faring. Heinrich's cards dangled carelessly from his left hand, his mouth was tight and his brow intent, facing the splintering wall of the boxcar as though lost in thought. Ivan looked up with an easy smile, his chains quietly clinking with the other knocks and clanks of the train.

Able took a deep breath and wrapping up his history of Mephisto rather quickly, he finished,

"Enough to say he began his youth, captured and oppressed,
Far different than how his life began, cast away, but blessed.

Of course, his life upon that ship did not fare so well,
I've heard tales of sad events I refuse to ever tell.

But I will tell you he was mistreated and so forced to mistreat,
And one day, so misused, he cracked and admitted his will was beat.
And he once told me something strange, I still don't fully understand.
He said, 'When I accepted I was broken, I then became a man.'"

After a moment of silence, Heinrich slowly came back to reality. The crate underneath him shook as the train clattered along and he wondered how long they had been traveling. He had utterly lost track of time. The story had seduced him again although in the end, it had taken a very unexpected tragic turn, and he began to doubt its veracity. He looked out the door and reviewed what he knew. Able had mentioned they were heading to a circus, and now he found out the leader, Mephisto, had been enslaved as a child. It did not seem likely, and he wondered how much of anything Able said was true, no matter how entertaining it was. Then, remembering one of the first things Able had mentioned, and feeling foolish for believing any of the tale since, he asked,

"Didn't you mention something about a mermaid?"

Chapter V
The Mermaid

Able perked up and said,

> *"Oh yes, of course, where have my thoughts been dwelling?*
> *On the darkest moments, not the parts I should be telling!"*

He twirled his mustache with a pinch and looked as though he were trying to figure out where he should begin. Then he snapped his fingers and picked up the tale at a point thirteen years later, as follows.

***

The figurehead, the very thing that had enticed him to board Rabar's cruel ship, became Mephisto's only solace during his long captivity. He developed a kinship with the sculpture along with the idea that she too was enslaved and used for evil when she could have stood for goodness. As the time ticked by, and the figurehead's veneer and beauty faded in the elements, Mephisto's spirit too became tired and worn. Many a night he crept to the bow to sit with her, his only friend, and as two forlorn prisoners, they would look into the dark unknown. He spoke aloud to her and once asked,

> *"Did I tempt my fate too much? Should I have stayed ashore?*
> *But I had no clues to direct my life. Woe that I asked for more."*

The figurehead always gave the same reply: silence. She never turned her head, even when, on the mistiest nights, tears welled in her wooden eyes and trickled down her cheeks. But Mephisto found consolation in her restraint, which he took for fortitude rather than coldness. She represented to him one who could see through all the tragedy and keep a lookout for a bright horizon, and was reminded of his own words when he had left the orphanage: *"I . . . always will be faithful, that life is good . . . "* With the figurehead as inspiration, he recognized his situation as only a test of his resolve, and renewed his trust that life was good, and that fate had led him to the figurehead, and thereby the ship, for a reason greater than pain.

On the thirteenth year of Mephisto's enslavement, him now twenty-three, the ship sailed into waters that it had not parted for two decades—waters only an old carpenter might recognize if he were still amongst the living (he died in his workshop, in his sleep, of old age shortly after carving the mermaid—he never jumped). In those waters, a special island breaks the surface: the island where mermaids dwell. Few have ever seen a mermaid because this island lies so far away and, to a greater extent, because it is guarded by a giant sea monster who is particularly protective of the mermaids. The monster swims around the island, always on the alert to detect any disturbance of a ship. If a ship ever steers close enough to see the island, and thereby any of the mermaids, or to hear their curious songs, the monster makes no considerations save one; leave no soul alive to bear witness of what it saw. Therefore, any surviving tales of mermaids are the result of a mermaid straying, unnoticed, beyond the monster's vigilance, and being spotted by a ship that has come close, but not close enough to be sensed by the beast—as had happened two decades past.

Rabar, Mephisto, and crew sailed straight for the island unaware. The monster's one giant eye sighted the pirates approaching its sacred boundary and gathered its mighty tentacles. However, a shark's length from the line of certain death, the ship changed course and headed away from the island, destined to pass by unmolested. The monster relaxed and also turned away, but as it began to sink into the dark depths, a realization dawned in its tiny mind: one of the mermaids had been mounted to the front of the ship, stiff and dry as though long dead. The monster stopped in a swirl of bubbles, then thrashed out its powerful limbs and rocketed through the brine.

Three times larger than a whale, the beast surged from the deep in an effervescent swell and rammed the offending vessel of mermaid murderers, nearly tipping it over and sending a wave of spray across the deck. The hull crunched fatally and the crew was thrown and washed into chaos. Two pirates sailed overboard and were immediately lost. The others crashed into the bulkheads, masts and each other. However, when they hit the deck, despite bruises and cracked ribs, they leapt to their feet and grabbed up harpoons, chains, anchors, swords, and anything else they could use as a weapon. As the ship righted itself, eight giant tentacles slowly rose into the air, taller than the masts, and hovered there. The crew held quiet as the swaying tentacles cast an ominous pattern of shadows over the decks. Without warning, the heavy fish flesh plummeted from its perilous height to pound and punish, and smashing the silence, it pummeled the deck.

"To war!" the pirates cried, undaunted.

Charging the beast from all directions like a swarm of angry hornets, the pirates gouged and hacked at the tentacles that lashed and dashed both vessel and men to pieces. The beast's razor fangs, the size of shark fins, gnashed at both the wooden bulwarks and flesh of man. Seeing an opportunity, one savage pirate grabbed a harpoon and stabbed at the beast's huge watery eye so that goo spewed forth. Another climbed the pearly slick skin of the beast and began to fillet the flesh. Pistols and cannons were fired until all the shot was buried in the monster's opalescent hide. Then, the cannons themselves were tied to harpoons embedded in the monster and dropped overboard to drag the beast to the bottom.

But the beast would not be easily overcome. Its tentacles readily flung men into the air like toys while leaving others crushed on the deck,

VI The Beast

gasping for air with broken lungs. Red dripped on the timber, red stained the sails, red sullied the sea. Mephisto climbed over the pitching deck and attempted to fortify gaping holes in the hull, but for every leak he dammed, the beast rent two. A bulkhead cracked to his right and splinters shot past his face. A line snapped and whipped through the air above him, slicing through a banister. A pirate screamed and a severed arm fell to the deck at Mephisto's feet. The hull groaned as its spine twisted and the timber cracked under the torture. The black flag and its laughing skull flew away in the breeze as the main mast burst apart with the swipe of a tentacle. A hush seemed to accompany the shadow of the mainsail as it slowly fell to the sea. All hope for victory, or that a man might stay alive, sank with it.

In the final moments of destruction, only two men remained. Rabar stood on the forecastle as it heaved and cracked, and holding a line with one hand, swung his seasoned sword with the other, slashing slimy limbs into retreat. Mephisto, on the quarterdeck, hacked the beast with two hand axes, until he realized that the more vigorous he cut, the more ferocious the enemy thrashed and flailed, and stopped his butchering. He almost cried a warning to Rabar, but hesitated, remembering all the wrong the captain had done him. *Any moment he will be destroyed,* he thought and pictured Rabar gasping for air, his lungs perforated by the fangs of the beast.

No, Mephisto decided, *I choose the man, not the beast,* (if he was referring to himself is debated) and called,

> *"Tragedy has found us Rabar, the more we fight the less we gain,*
> *For every blow, the beast strikes two; your aggressions are in vain.*
> *We don't understand this enemy, fighting makes our stance more grim.*
> *I don't know the way to beat it, but it's not by wasting life and limb.*
>
> *Perhaps if we stop fighting we can make it out alive,*
> *Lash yourself to some floatation and you may yet survive.*
> *Let us agitate the beast no more; let us be unseen amongst the wreck,*
> *Your fury and fight are worthless now! This is a truth you must accept!"*

Rabar's dark hair dripped with sea and sweat. He made a mighty swing, cleaving a tentacle in two and goo spilled forth. He spat a tooth into it, inhaled deeply, and roared,

"The truth? Young fool, if that be it, I'll not accept it,
I shall fight against defeat, and if I die, I'll not regret it.
I will have fought with all I have, though I may receive the final blow,
I will not abandon this wretched ship to accept a fate I do not know!

And who are you to give advice? Look what fate has done for you,
Life doesn't just work out! Look at the misery hope has put you through.

Yet still you trust blind faith and chance, you won't put up a fight,
Then run again and waste your life, go slip quietly into the night!
You were an ungrateful runaway and look what you became,
A yellow-bellied, craven coward! **Go and die ashamed!"**

The sea roiled and churned as the creature's thrashing dismantled the ship. Planks burst, slicing through clouds of salt water spray. The ocean surged in through massive breaches and shot through cracks in the deck like fountains until the deck burst with a great erupting geyser, throwing the men apart. Mephisto crashed into the helm and his ribs broke. Bits of the creature, water, and debris swirled around him like a nightmare. He pushed up to his knees and saw scarlet blood pooling underneath him. He gasped as sweat, tears, and sea stung his eyes. His vision darkened and he screamed at Rabar, though he could not see him,

"You're not a fighter, you are defeated! How can you not know?
You gave up the real fight, the fight for good, far too long ago!
There are other ways, but you are too afraid to find your fate!
You are a wicked man who has replaced his hope with hate.

You fight to conquer demons, but find there are ever more,
Can't you see you find just what you are looking for?
Search for life instead, leave this demon. Why are you afraid?
Do you fear you will succeed? Do you curse how you were made?

So curse you, not I! You are the fool; now death may have this day,
But, if not, may this moment inspire us to live our lives a different way!
If I live . . . I will live unafraid . . . I will so live so all can see,
I am not ashamed of who I am or what I'm designed to be!"

Mephisto collapsed. Fighting fading consciousness, he crawled amongst the destruction towards the bow of the ship. He had to swim across a gape where the deck was destroyed and pulled himself onto the forecastle until he reached the one thing that had buoyed his faith that redemption would come. Alas, the figurehead was knocked loose and no longer faced the horizon; she looked ahead as staunchly as ever, but into the dark depths of the sea. Mephisto's life-light flickered, so did his faith, and he was finally broken. He wrapped his arms around the figurehead, his blood streamed down the wood, and he whispered,

"You were my sign and made me think I had a special destiny,
But I was wrong, all along; life is unhappiness and treachery.
I hoped it would give me a purpose, but I misunderstood,
Life is random misery; now I must close my eyes for good."

As he closed his eyes, several mermaids, having heard the commotion of the battle, swam out from the island to witness the destruction. They dodged pieces of the ship sinking around them as they gawked at the bodies floating on the churning surface. A mermaid with long red hair caught sight of a curiously familiar silhouette. She dared to swim a bit closer to the surface and found the silhouette to be a giant wooden version of herself floating face down as though searching for something in the expanse of the sea. After checking that her sisters weren't watching, she grabbed a rope dangling from the sculpture and began to hurry it back toward the island.

As the mermaid approached the coast, she headed for a blue light, ten feet underwater, that revealed an opening through the cliffs—a passageway not visible above the surface. She towed the sculpture through this narrow passage, cringing each time her rope went tight and she heard the figurehead scraping the rocks. She pulled from below, fighting surging swells, as barnacles and rock chipped away and sank around her. At last, she broke through a dense forest of seaweed and the figurehead passed the gauntlet of rocks above. The water transformed into a sparkling aqua blue with patterns of light weaving a loose alternating tapestry on the sandy lagoon floor. The shadow beneath her showed that she still had her treasure. Triumphant, she kicked her tail until she arrived at a small hidden beach. Vines with leaves as broad as sunfish hung like an upside down kelp forest from an overhanging grotto, offering her a curtain of privacy.

She heaved the figurehead into the shallows and began to examine the damage. Golden light streaming through the vines revealed only small gouges marring the wooden surface, some paint chipped away, and part of the tail splintered off. She ran her fingers over the smooth designs of the sculpture's face as she touched her own delicate cheeks and lips. It was so similar. She entertained the naive idea that the figurehead was the mold she herself had been modeled from. With white webbed fingers, she untied the tangles of rigging that obscured parts of the sculpture. As she pulled a large knot free, the lines yanked from her hands and a dark form tumbled off the back of the sculpture onto the shore. The mermaid splashed back with a powerful thrust of her tail, but after a moment's pause, the form remaining motionless, she approached. She brushed her wet hair from her eyes and found the body of a man lying with his face smashed into the sand, three inches underwater. She pushed, rolled, and dragged him onto the beach where she examined his face with her cold fingertips and peeled back his eyelids. A foreign feeling overwhelmed her: a combination of longing and loss for something she had never known. She leaned down and pressed her lips against those of Mephisto.

VII The Grotto

Chapter VI
The Arrival

Able finished his tale with a clap of his hands,

"Her kiss made him revive,
It's love that keeps that man alive!"

Heinrich snorted and slapped his shaking forehead.

"That has got to be the wildest tall tale I've ever heard," he said. Able laughed and replied,

"Don't be so quick to define what you cannot know,
Do you already draw the line between what is real and what is show?
How then do you propose you could ever learn something new?
Believe what you want, of course, but every word is true."

"Okay, I'm sorry. I didn't mean it that way," Heinrich said, uncertain if Able was joking. Able nodded and looked back at his cards.

"Is it really true?" Heinrich asked. He couldn't help it. He knew it wasn't true, but he had to know if Able believed the story or not. He needed to know if he was dealing with an insane person.

Able looked up in disbelief.

"Okay, just kidding," Heinrich laughed. He decided Able was definitely a madman and this renewed his concern of whether he was telling the truth about anything. Was the train really going to a circus? And if so, and these two strange men were part of it, should he be alarmed? In any case, he was alarmed. The train was still moving way too fast to jump. *Just go with it, Heinrich,* he told himself. *Able is just having fun.*

"Can I ask," he asked, "how this Mephisto made it back here without a ship?"

Without missing a beat, Able replied,

"Heinrich! Who cares the how? Though, what could be more plain?
On the back of the mermaid, did that really need to be explained?

Each brought to this country a prize in the other, and also one together,
For as he was carried, Mephisto carried a chest of pirate treasure."

Heinrich snorted with disbelief again, but Able nodded encouragingly,

"It's okay. It's wild, I know. You can take heart,
A lot of other people have asked about that part."

Heinrich let it go and smiled. He didn't think Able was making fun of him, but also couldn't believe Able believed his stories. He seemed too reasonable. In any case, the story had passed the time wonderfully and just then the jostling of the boxcar lessened, the clacking quieted, and the fields outside rushed past in less of a hurry. Bottlebrush grass and blue harebell flowers crowded toward the tracks. About half a mile away a town stood in a dusty haze. Between the train and the town, a broad encampment of canvas tents stood in the plains, the grass trampled down or cleared away. Slender poles waving triangular flags surrounded the encampment at intervals and supported strings of electric lights. Several two-horse caravans stood along one edge of the lot, a few containing lumber and rope, but most with smokestacks, windows, and ornate decorations in the woodwork. Along the opposite edge of the lot, parked trucks were being unloaded by men hurrying back and forth between the various pavilions. The train eased to a stop about fifty yards from the encampment as the brakes let out a hiss of relief having convinced the wheels to cease their rolling. Bright balloons and banners above the tents eliminated one of Heinrich's doubts. The destination was real. They were at a circus.

ACT TWO
Before The Show

Chapter I
Karl The Strong

Like poking a stick in an anthill, the train's arrival provoked a flurry of action. Roustabouts and circus hands rushed from the tents, kicking up a dust cloud along the entire length of the train. They slid open the boxcars and lugged out a seemingly endless stream of crates and barrels, and hauled scaffolding, poles, and painted signs off the flatbed cars. The commotion of the offloading was nearly louder than the train had been. Heinrich leaned out from the doorway and was amazed to see trainers escort show horses, donkeys, giraffes and zebras from the train. Near the back of the train, he saw some large cages being carefully guided down gradual ramps. A lion paced in one cage and a leopard slept in another, while a giant crocodile's tail protruded from the bars of the last.

Without waiting for his traveling companions, Heinrich hopped to the ground only to reel back as a workman charged by him, climbed into the boxcar and began to unstack the crates. Heinrich pressed his back against the hot train and wondered how he could weave his way through the hustle and bustle. He realized he didn't even have to go to the circus; he could head out into the plains again. He glanced back at his two companions as Able tossed a key to Ivan, who proceeded to unlock his shackles. The two swung down from the car and Able smacked his hands together, grinning, while Ivan let out a sigh, and the two headed along the train towards the tents. With no great plan decided on, Heinrich followed, trying to not lose them in the crowd.

As they strolled past the hissing engine, Heinrich looked up and squinted for the blinding white paint. Behind the massive steam drum, in the shadow of the large smoke stack, the engineer sat in his small cab, crowded by handles, greasy pipes and quivering dials. His gray whiskers were swept to one side like a puff of smoke in the wind. Coal dust underscored the creases in his face and arms, making them look like cracks in a fractured China doll. From his experience in the mines, Heinrich knew how hard coal dust was to clean off, especially after it had baked in with sweat. His father used to leave for work in the morning with dark lines still on his face from the previous day. Though the locomotive had stopped, the engineer's hands and head still shook like a sputtering engine, causing his pipe to rattle against his teeth. Slumping shoulders and heavy eyelids suggested he had long since grown accustomed to the twitching.

What a life, Heinrich thought and wondered how much the engineer had seen, sitting up front, watching everything speed by. The engineer, as though sensing someone watching him, began to turn his shaking head. Heinrich couldn't turn away, even as it became evident that the engineer was turning toward him. When the engineer's head finally completed its spasmodic turn, he focused on Heinrich and said in a raspy voice,

> *"When the hard times come, know this to be true,*
> *The good times only taught me vice, the bad times only virtue."*

The engineer's eyelids and shaky head bowed. Heinrich nodded back. The engineer was likely running out of steam himself, he reasoned, but couldn't help wondering what he meant about hard times coming. The engineer faced ahead again and began whistling a hollow, sad tune which made Heinrich consider that he must be a virtuous man.

He spotted Able and Ivan thirty yards ahead and ran to catch up, only to find Ivan walking away. Ivan turned back, holding his scarred head high, and waved farewell. *Whatever his job is, he's bound to frighten someone*, Heinrich thought. Able looked at the train engine and gave Heinrich a questioning look. Heinrich just shrugged, not sure what to say. Able laughed,

> *"He's just old, trying to understand what he's been through,*
> *Some folks give advice when it's just themselves they're talking to."*

The sun continued its climb toward the pinnacle of the pale blue sky. Able gestured in the direction of the circus and offered Heinrich a tour of the grounds. Despite many of the tents being only half raised and the general commotion of construction, there were groups of other visitors strolling about the circus. Able explained that although the circus officially opened the following day, the townsfolk are allowed a preview as the spectacle is assembled and the performers rehearse. Able also mentioned, to Heinrich's surprise, that the circus would only perform for one day, but he assured that it was not to be missed as it was truly a life changing event.

They passed a ticket booth in construction and approached a small stage with a wagon as both backdrop and backstage. Two rosy-cheeked, robust dancing girls followed an older man dressed as the devil, in red tights, a cape, a goatee and horns on his head. He was sternly pointing to markings on the stage floor with his pitchfork, and waiting as the ladies twirled from mark to mark in his prescribed order. To the left of the wagon, two men in bowler hats and bowties bowed together and tuned a standing bass with a banjo, while another man raked his fingertips across a washboard. On other stages, set designers arranged props and fixed any damage incurred from transportation. Painted jugglers and acrobats on stilts walked through the crowds. A flock of young ladies in feather costumes fluttered into a tent. In the shade, a man in stripes breathed fire as his lady counterpart twirled it at the end of chains. A procession of camels draped with embroidered blankets and tassels, loped by without a guide.

Heinrich's attention whipped one way and then another like that of a starving man stumbling into a bazaar. Meticulous carvings and exotic designs adorned the booths and stages. Palm trees in large decorated urns were being placed to line the main thoroughfare. Banners promising wonders from *The Alligator Man* to *The Floating Mummy of the Nile* billowed their wild illustrations in the breeze. A woman sat still as a marble statue, displaying black tattoos covering every inch of her exposed skin like the markings on a treasure map. Two ladies draped with silk undulated ample abdomens like genies wriggling out of lamps. A bow-tied magician concentrated on a white tipped wand as it danced between his hands. Streamers and colored lanterns decorated the sky.

Incredible, Heinrich thought. These people were as colorful and varied as the insects and birds he'd observed as a boy. The amount of preparation for a show that would last only a day amazed him and reminded him of the life of a butterfly. Some of the smaller species only live a couple days, most have but a couple weeks to display their delicate glory. Not

VIII Rehearsal

long at all, especially considering the amount of preparation they make. He remembered one of the first times nature had fascinated him. His father had pointed out two chrysalises on a branch of a milkweed plant on the back porch. Days later, Heinrich had found a pipevine swallowtail exercising its dark blue wings for the first time. The second chrysalis remained perfectly whole with the butterfly's wings visible through the transparent shell, but after another week it had started to wither and Heinrich had to accept that the butterfly would never make it out. The chrysalis had been a womb for one and a tomb for the other.

A boisterous group of spectators brought Heinrich's thoughts back to the present. They were gathered shoulder to shoulder, obscuring an attraction from view. Heinrich and Able peered between the collection of derbies, fedoras, and flowered hats to see, in a space made by the encircling crowd, a strongman in a red leotard, boots, and a wide belt, lifting impossible weights. He hefted a cart axle, with two barrels of sand lashed to either end, above his head with one hand as if he was just checking the inclination of the breeze. His powerful muscles were taut, and yet he had the easiest smile.

The strongman lifted barbells marked with a one and several zeros with equally apparent ease. Two men from the crowd tried to pick a single barbell up and could not have had a harder time if they'd tried to stop the Earth from spinning. The small crowd gasped and sighed at each feat of strength, and the strongman's smile never wavered. Then he lifted a dusty little girl in his hand, her little boots in his palm, as though she were as light as a dandelion flower turned to seed. Her eyes went wide as she rose into the air, but seeing her parents, she giggled and waved. The strongman spoke with a voice that matched his physique,

> *"I am Karl the Strong, and I love lifting things up high,*
> *I continue to lift even greater things, every time I try.*
> *But being greatly strong is not the greatest thing I do,*
> *I bear my burdens gratefully because I lift spirits too!"*

XI The Painted Lady

A smile spread across Heinrich's face. *You don't need so many muscles to make someone's day,* he thought, *and this fellow has far too many, but what better thing to do with them?* Any concerns he had about how and why he'd come to be at a circus, lessened as though lifted away.

X Karl The Strong

Chapter II
The Falconess

Maybe hopping the train wasn't such a bad idea, after all, Heinrich thought. The circus performers were not all runaways and conmen like he'd always thought. Able tugged his sleeve, hinting at plenty more to see. Sure enough, near a small booth in which an old man was hanging glass baubles for sale, they discovered another crowd.

A young lady, costumed in a forest green dress, stood at the center of attention. A leather glove adorned her right hand, and various small purses hung from her belt. Next to her, a proud eagle and a hunched vulture perched on a wooden stand with three perches; the third stood noticeably empty. The falconess held up her right hand and the eagle jumped, flapped its broad wings twice, reached out its talons, and landed on her glove. She rewarded it with a morsel from one of her purses, then extended her arm and encouraged members of the audience to hold out their hands. A young boy stared in awe at the eagle but held close to his mother's dress as it was brought near. The falconess knowingly smiled and gently guided the eagle to step onto the boy's shoulder. The boy cringed, but as the eagle settled, his demeanor shifted from fear to proud bravery.

Suddenly, to everyone's alarm, the eagle's head jerked completely around, focusing its yellow eyes on Heinrich, and it let out a piercing shriek. The falconess whipped around too, and spying Heinrich, her eyes narrowed like the bird's as she warned,

"The falcon does not hear the call. It is out of touch and drifting.
It waits for the right breeze to blow, but the winds are ever shifting."

XI The Falconess

The crowd leaned inward and stared at Heinrich. He couldn't make any sense out of the girl's cryptic speech. The falconess took a step forward, pointing with her glove. Her tone grew more serious,

> *"You cannot catch the wind; you cannot change its pace,*
> *You cannot stop the years as they blow cracks across your face.*
> *Cast your fate into that wind . . . before it disappears,*
> *Let it take you where it will and blow away your fears.*
>
> *The right path is what you choose, why are you hesitating?*
> *Nothing is under one's control; there is no use in waiting."*

Heinrich anxiously looked over his shoulders both for Able and to indicate to the crowd that he had no idea why this performer was singling him out. The falconess continued staring at him as he edged backward.

"Okay, Okay," he laughed nervously. The little boy with the eagle on his shoulder began to whimper, looking at his mother and too afraid to move. Finally, Able grabbed Heinrich's arm and rescued him from the scene. Once in the clear, Able reassured him,

> *"Don't worry, she's upset; that was a little out of hand,*
> *I believe she's missing something; did you see the empty stand?*
> *Come, let's move along, there is much more at this fair,*
> *Up ahead, another person searching, just look over there."*

Heinrich clutched Able's shoulder ready to forget what had just happened, and looked where Able pointed. A woman stood on a stage styled like a western saloon. Behind her stood a cream dresser with a pot of flowers on top, a calico upholstered chair, and an upright piano. Yellowing, patterned wallpaper peeled from the back wall. But it was the woman herself, twirling a pink parasol, that looked completely out of place.

"What a costume!" Heinrich remarked, "Who thinks of this stuff?"
Able paused and looking at Heinrich, shook his head and said,

"I am afraid that is no costume. Mephisto met her way out west,
Hers is a curious story . . . Let me tell you of her quest."

Chapter III
The Lady

Heinrich was happy for the diversion and, he had to admit, to hear another one of Able's stories. He recalled the last story ending ridiculously with Mephisto riding across the ocean on the back of a mermaid. Having arrived at a circus, after all, he guessed that maybe Able worked as a story teller here. He thought about asking, but Able was already talking. Here is the story he told.

***

Mephisto returned to the mainland thirteen years from when he'd left it, and clueless as to what part of the coast he and the mermaid had arrived at. On a scouting mission, he entered the nearest town and realized it was now nearly as foreign to him as it would be to the mermaid. Eager to explore, and with an unbreakable bond made during their adventure across the sea, and also an immense treasure, they decided to discover the ways of the country together.

Mephisto retrofitted a horse-drawn gypsy caravan to house them as they traveled. He strengthened the axles and framework to bear the weight of a large internal water tank. Using thick glass, he built the tank as tall as his chest along one half of the caravan, permitting room for the mermaid to stretch out in. He installed a lip around the edge to prevent the water from splashing over the rest of the interior which included a narrow bed for himself, a stove and a set of cupboards. In the caravan wall against the tank, he fitted two portals so the mermaid could look out or close and hide from strangers—which was everyone. A crate of tools and horse tackle were stowed on a small porch by the door.

For five years, the two traveled everywhere the caravan could take them. They only required to stop by a river, preferably one with a waterfall, or the sea, each month to change out the water in the tank, take a swim, and fish, the latter of which the mermaid proved particularly good at. On the road, Mephisto often rode the horse to watch for dangers and dismounted to lead the horse and caravan over rough terrain. However, he preferred to steer from the front of the caravan where he could point out every amazing thing to his love, and hear her exclamations of surprise with each new discovery, which included a great many fascinating individuals.

By the end of their travels, the interior, which had begun as bare wood and a few bed sheets, sparkled with trinkets, lanterns, and glass figurines. Purple and turquoise silk covered the ceiling, flashing with the movement of the caravan, like the pitching surface of the ocean. Tassels hung from it like jellyfish. Handcrafted brass cookware hung above the stove. Lavender and jasmine flowers filled vases on the cupboards, and the air with a floral scent to mix with the vanilla incense Mephisto burned in the evenings. His simple bed had changed. It could not be seen for a proliferation of pillows, embroidered throws, and calico sheets. The mermaid, enamored with the delicate patterns of calico, always requested another example when they neared a town.

During one of their last journeys in the west, the journey that convinced Mephisto to use the pirate treasure to start the circus, he parked the caravan next to a trickling stream in a wide golden plain where the smell of sweet pea flowers floated in the air. A young boy exploring the stream saw the caravan and consequently, two miles away and an hour later, word of the curious caravan spread through a small town. In this town, a poor beggar woman lived amongst the boxes, newspapers, and rats of a dark alley. She hid away for most of the day, only crawling to the sidewalk, scraping her knees, with her head bowed and hands extended for spare change, for a couple hours each afternoon. The people who walked past her, and generally ignored her and put no money in her hands, discouraging her shameful behavior and encouraging her to go away, that day gave her something far more valuable than coin. Two women leaving the grocery store dropped a priceless piece of gossip about a traveling caravan into her ear, which was just the change she needed.

She crawled back to the alley and stood up. She smoothed the front of her stained dress, brushing off bits of trash, and picked cigarette butts out of her hair. Then she adjusted her hat, retied the scarf always around her face, and did something she had not done in the six months since arriving in town: she *walked* from the alley shadows. She cleared her voice, startling herself with a sound like a cat coughing up a hair-ball, then walked over to a man reading a newspaper at the bus stop.

"Have you heard the news of the traveler?" she asked. The man responded without looking up from his paper,

"The one with the strange caravan?"

"Yes, that one. Is he nearby?"

"At the old Shannon farm, I've heard. The place was abandoned after the old man and son died in the war."

The woman paused, affected by the comment. She took a deep breath and asked,

"How far is the farm?"

"Oh just east a couple miles." The man folded his paper. "I was thinkin' about heading out there to have a look myself if you'd like to come al..."

Suddenly, upon seeing the beggar woman, the man leaped up, backed away, and put the bench between himself and the woman. He shook his newspaper at her with one hand as he dug in his pockets with the other and threw a few coins down the alley.

"There you go! Go on and leave me be!" he shouted.

But the woman was already leaving, and not in the direction of the coins. She was looking for something more valuable than money, and travelers know where many things are.

The woman stepped up the small stairs of Mephisto's caravan and knocked on the door. After some shifting and the sound of splashing water, Mephisto, now a tall bearded man, opened the door a crack and peered out from bluish shadows. He beheld the poor woman in a ruined dress that had once been fine. She was holding a dirty scarf tightly around her face, hiding all but beautiful, sad eyes. *Once, she must have had everything sewn up tight,* he thought, *but something has torn the seams.* The lady lowered her chin, obscuring her face with the brim of her hat. Mephisto said nothing. A light breeze whispered in the dry grass. The lady broke the quiet at last,

"Have you been traveling long?" she asked.

Mephisto replied mystically,

"My lady, I've seen seven great oceans and have traveled every sea, There is not a land too far, nor tribe of people still unknown to me.

I have tasted the oddest delicacies, watched rituals that would warp your mind. I've been deep in the darkest forests and to the further reaches of time.

And as I've traveled to unknown parts of this great land, I have been to the hidden plains that lie in the heart of man."

He paused briefly, looking down his long nose at the lady. She looked at him despite herself and quickly looked down again. He predicted,

"You sought me out for I have ventured further than you've dared before, So sit you down and tell me who you are and what you're looking for."

Mephisto slipped out the caravan door, closed it, and motioned for the lady to lead the way to two wooden chairs in the dirt. A sound like a latch opening came from the caravan and Mephisto gestured again for the lady to have a seat. She obeyed and subsequently drew a ragged black and white photograph from her dress and handed it to him.

"*My name is Mary, if you please,*" she said, "*and the man in the photograph is Ulysses.*" After a swift glance, Mephisto handed the photo back. He had never seen the man. He said,

> "*As I feared when I opened my door, in your bearing I'd seen enough,*
> *You search for a great treasure gone. You have lost the one you love.*
> *What I know of this man is only that which I now see in your eyes,*
> *He is someone you hold very dear, your husband I'll surmise.*
>
> *Where could he be? The tragedy has left you desolate and poor,*
> *I judge by his age in this photograph that he may have gone to war.*
> *If so, my dear, allow with my sincerest regret,*
> *There may be a grim reality you have yet to accept,*"

Mary glanced down and said,

> "*It is so, he went to war, and since that day I've held my breath,*
> *But I am in a position to know, Ulysses has not met with death.*"

Mephisto leaned in and eyed the lady. She had still not removed the dirty scarf from her face. Crafting a plan, he retrieved a jug of water and two thick glasses from a crate behind his chair. Pouring a glass, he handed it the lady but she refused it. Mephisto kept the glass of water in front of her and spoke,

> "*I offer you this drink, but you think it an ordeal,*
> *I believe you hide a secret, one you hope to not reveal.*
> *For to drink from this cup, you must remove your wrap,*
> *I now suspect, it would pain you to do that.*
>
> *For I declare, beneath you hide some deformity,*
> *Of which you are ashamed, one you would not have me see!*"

XII The Caravan

Mary let out a pitiful moan and admitted,

"There is an unhappy way I know Ulysses remains alive,
It began on the day he left, and it has been my demise.
My longing for him brought about an awful curse,
Which I cannot be rid of, and each day it just gets worse.

It's my sad connection to him, my miserable relief,

I know he lives for if he did not, I believe the curse would cease.
And though I would then be cured of my wretched shame,
I would only suffer all the more knowing he's been claimed.

If only I could see him again, two blessings would I gain,
My emptiness would abandon me and with it would go my bane."

Mephisto's heart broke for this woman, abandoned by her love, but he still did not fully understand her plight. He stood and demanded,

"I have seen a great many things, I cannot be upset,
What is this curse you suffer? You have not revealed that yet.
Show me this proof he is alive; remove that scarf about your neck,
Show me this affliction you fear that I will not accept!"

Mary's light blue eyes began to tear. She turned away and undid the scarf covering her face. When she turned back and looked directly at Mephisto, his hand rose so sharply he slapped his beard.

"Poor lady! You are a beauty, but for this sadness unrestrained,
I can see the wildness of unrequited love that can't be tamed.
You must find closure or resolution, a way to cure this pain:
Either he dies or he returns, or you never think of him again!"

Then, realizing he had become too passionate, Mephisto softened,

"Alas, none of these things have happened, allow me to propound,
We must take a course of action so that your Ulysses can be found.
I may have a plan, something I've devised,
A traveling show for folks like you, where nothing is disguised.

If you are willing to risk everything, to step into the light and be exposed,
I have a strategy that will allow you to search for him everywhere we go.

I shall take you far and wide, at least that much I can give,
For there is nothing worse than to forget a man who lives.

You must be ready to dismiss what people say and ignore every reaction,
While we search for your Ulysses, you'll use your curse as an attraction!"

***

Heinrich gawked. The performer, wearing a pink dress like a lady, and holding a parasol like a lady, sported a full beard, very much not like a lady. Her nose was delicate, her cheeks high, both spattered with light freckles. Long, rich brown tresses were bundled under a wide pink hat. If not for the strange aspect of facial hair, and her looking so forlorn, she would be very beautiful.

The Bearded Lady scanned each new face in the crowd as though she was indeed, looking for someone like her long lost Ulysses. Her gaze rested on Heinrich's face, then darted off again unfazed. The reality, Heinrich thought, was more likely that the lady was worried about being recognized working such a bizarre job, and she was hoping *not* to find anyone she knew. Even so, her tale and beard surely as false as the rest of Able's stories, Heinrich, just for fun, entertained the idea that her story was real. His imagination running away with him, he began to feel sorry for her loss and her condition. Real or fake, he became indignant and a little embarrassed at how he and the crowd gawked at her

"Look how the people just stare," he said to Able."She can't be happy. She's up there like a freak."

Able smiled knowingly and replied,

"But there she is Heinrich, on display, attracting folks far and wide,
So Ulysses may come to see the Bearded Lady that would be his bride.
And though he would never know her, and pass by the oddity rejected,
She is diligent in her searching. He could not pass by undetected.

XIII The Bearded Lady

From her stage, she can see it all, though it may seem rather grim,
Know that if ever he does come to see her, she will see him!
Understand this, what others think does not matter in the end,
It is not about her looks or how they look, it is she who looks at them!"

Chapter IV
The Gypsy

Able winked and walked away. Heinrich hesitated. *What would I do if I just didn't care what other people thought?* he wondered. *Not work at the mine? Hike through forests looking for birds all day?* That seemed about as unrealistic as this lady's act. But despite not coming up with an answer as to what he might do, he appreciated the question and the exhibit that had inspired it. Then he realized that, since hopping the train, there had been several incidents that had caused him to wonder about his own life, as though they'd been directed at him specifically, and this gave rise to the strangest inkling that there was more to the circus and it all might mean something.

The heat of midday and the dust of the crowds created a haze that tempered the brilliance of the blue sky. The breeze had disappeared along with the long shadows of morning. The canvas tents bathed in the sunlight and became indistinct in the dust while rainbow balloons, fluorescent lollipops, and painted signs popped with vibrant colors. Smoke rose from a stand decorated with yellow stripes and the smell of sausages and onions on the grill wafted through the air, making Heinrich's tongue tingle. He hadn't eaten all day, in fact, the hobo had disrupted his morning before he'd even had coffee. Able walked over to the stand and as the two waited in line, a boy at the condiments counter forked a heap of sauerkraut onto a sausage as his mother waited. She looked concerned with how much the boy was taking, though not for his health as it turned out, she wanted just as much. Beyond the counter, off the main thoroughfare, past ribbons and balloons, a metal sculpture in the shape of an eye, on the peak of a tent, glinted. Heinrich pointed out the eye and the tent to Able. Able tilted his head and shrugged his shoulders.

"Good eye, but I've never seen that tent before,
How can that be? How can there be one more?"

"Let's find out," said Heinrich.

After filling up on sauerkraut, the two slipped away from the crowds. They approached the tent and discovered a young girl in a checkered cape seated on a bale of hay. She hummed a quiet tune while she piled pieces of grass on her little knees. She did not look up as Heinrich approached so he passed by without disturbing her. When Able followed, she reacted and jumped up holding out her hand, palm forward. Able stopped in his tracks. The girl said nothing but leveled a serious glare at him. Heinrich thought it comical at first, but after a few moments of Able standing there, he became anxious.

Then the little performer glanced over her shoulder in the direction of a man leaning against a pole at the side of the tent. He wore an ill-fitting coat that had more patches than fabric, loose brown pants, shoes full of holes and white paint decorating his face. The girl snapped and waved at the man, but he did not react; he just watched as curious as any spectator. The girl pouted and frowned at him, then turned to face Able again. She kept her hand up, planted her other hand on her waist and seemed even more determined to prevent Able from proceeding.

"We can leave," Heinrich offered. "We don't have to see what's inside this tent."

Able thought for a second then said,

"Believe me, but for her hand, there is nothing in my way,
Perhaps I'm not restrained, but rather, shown that I can stay.

XIV A Curious Child

Perhaps I should not go in, some things are better left unknown,
Or perhaps the child indicates that you go on alone.

Perhaps something will be shown to you; perhaps it is a sign,
If not us, or me, then you, go see whatever you would find."

Heinrich did not want to part ways with Able. The man knew his way around. However, Able was encouraging him to check out the tent. *What harm could come from taking a peek inside?* Heinrich reasoned.

"Okay, wait for me." he said.

Heinrich parted the canvas door, letting loose a cloud of mildew and dust. The material felt like it might disintegrate at his fingertips. As he stepped in, goosebumps raised on his arms with a significant drop in temperature. His vision adjusted to the darkness and revealed a candle flickering in heavy fog. A bookcase, its shelves stuffed with heavy tomes and dusty scrolls, lurked into view. A tall cabinet loomed in a corner. A shelf with earthen jars and glass bottles containing colored powders and dried herbs materialized on his right. Tapestries hung down from the dark space of the roof. As he inched further in, the fog dissipated, revealing a soft greenish glow coming from a crystal orb on a little table covered with a lace tablecloth. A woman hunched behind the orb. She reached out with a bony hand and gestured for Heinrich to sit down.

She wore a patterned scarf wrapped around her head with a jewel at the front. A shawl draped over her skeletal shoulders. Golden bracelets, gemstone rings, and crystal necklaces ornamented her arms, fingers, and neck. Her dress looked like a variety of carpets and curtains sewn together. A smile cracked her wrinkled face like a walnut splitting open. Heinrich, uncomfortable in the dark closed-in space, looked back, but couldn't see where he'd entered the tent. He took a breath and sat down in the wooden chair opposite the woman.

The woman leaned over the crystal sphere and as her face was illuminated by the glow of the orb, he saw that one of her eyes was made of wood. It had been painted white and marked with a blue spot in the center. The wooden eye did not move in unison with her real eye, which watched Heinrich. After a few squints and grunts, the gypsy nodded and her face retreated from the orb as she sat back down. She began to speak with a raspy voice,

> *"Welcome at last dear Heinrich. Surprised I know your name?*
> *Look around you, isn't it clear? I can see the future in a flame.*
> *I am Leonora the gypsy. I've been expecting you, poor soul,*
> *My part upon this stage is to help you to find your role."*

Heinrich had to admit he was impressed and he had just wondered if there was something more to the circus. He leaned in. The gypsy continued,

> *"Mysteries surround us, things you do not understand,*
> *How do I know your name? Why is Able banned?*
> *The falconess called you out, but her reason is unclear,*
> *Are you significant? Is there a reason you are here?*
>
> *It was not an accident that you hopped aboard the train.*
> *The accident was you stranded out in the wayward plains.*
> *Heinrich, you have a purpose, call it an opportunity,*
> *To allow and to accept how you were designed to be."*

Heinrich fidgeted with his chair. *How does she know I hopped the train?* he wondered. *Did Able slip her information somehow? No way.*

"What was I designed to be?" he asked.

The bent gypsy rose from her chair again. The crystal orb dimmed as dark smoke mysteriously swirled within it. She spoke in a grave way,

> *"These are the testing grounds, a crucible of great extremes,*
> *The place to hammer and temper your spirit in between,*

To chip away the dirt and grime, so you may hone,
A crystal, amongst the fire and the roughest stone.
This is the place where you can make it all shine true,
And should you succeed, there will be no limits left for you.

If you fail, you'll not be punished, you'll not be spurned,
You'll remain unaware why you suffer, too afraid to learn.

The testing grounds are full of wonder, but also so much pain,
But, for its onerous trials, the truth will be made plain,
The way to make it through, the way you will succeed,
You must accept yourself to find how you were made to be."

The gypsy, having become rather agitated, settled back down. Her good eye zeroed in on Heinrich as the wooden eye lolled at the crystal ball.

"Trust what you will see here, be it joy or be it terror,
Take your chances, The Fantastic Strange won't last forever."

The mystic stopped and pointed. Her ancient finger, drooping with the weight of sparkling rings, indicated the tall cabinet in the corner. She gave Heinrich a concerned look that reminded him of his old boss Harris. *What is going on?* he wondered. A scarlet draw curtain concealed an opening in the cabinet. The gypsy pointed firmly at it, causing her bracelets to jangle. *Let's get this act over with,* thought Heinrich. He approached the cabinet, wiped the sweat from his neck and onto his pants. He pulled the curtain aside.

What he saw caused the blood to drain from his face and his chest to tremble. His breath caught in his throat and he gagged. Tears streamed down his cheeks and he felt dizzy. He stumbled backward and almost tripped over his chair, a twisting pain in his stomach dropped him to his knees.

"What is that?" he wheezed, "Why did you show me that?"

The swirling mist closed in and Heinrich's vision blurred and

XV Leonora The Gypsy

doubled. The cabinet seemed to become two, then triple and begin to spin. He was delirious and nausea overwhelmed him. He gripped his abdomen, jumped up and bolted headlong out of the tent. The gypsy leapt from her chair and screamed after him,

> *"Because you looked, because you looked! Accept what you have found,*
> *Or you will be found wanting! Wanting in the testing grounds!"*

Chapter V
The Wolfman

Heinrich staggered through a maze of tents and lines reaching out like a spider web. Blinded by panic, he stumbled, knocked over a barrel, and lurched to the ground. Soft grass cushioned his cheekbone as it struck the earth, but his jaw twisted painfully. Lying on his front and looking to his side, he saw a tent stake sticking a foot out of the ground, inches away from his skull. A bright point of light quivered before his eyes. Tiny, white hepatica flowers poked out of the dirt like little fireworks. *What is this place*, he thought, *this place of wonder and so much pain?*

The sunlight and fresh air began to ease his nerves and he regained his senses. He understood that he had just been spooked by a frightening prop, some sort of grotesque mask, behind the curtain of the gypsy's cabinet, and she had set him on edge with her fortune telling act. The gypsy, of course, had ways of finding out secrets, he reasoned. That's why she had a circus act. He shook his head and let out a sheepish laugh. *Curse me for being the fool who allows himself deceived*, he said to himself. *It just entertainment, like Able's stories and the Bearded Lady. How could it all mean something? Try to have fun.*

His stomach no longer hurt and his breathing returned to normal. He picked himself up, dusted his pants and walked back to the midway where the bustle of the crowd comforted him. The fear retreated like a nightmare until he couldn't even recall it, and he became distracted searching the crowd, hoping to spot Able.

A roar like that of a wounded lion and the gasp of a crowd grabbed his attention. The crowd surrounded a large, tall wagon which resembled a cage, as it had jail bars in place of walls. Giving a reason for the high security, a beast inside the cage, standing eight feet tall on its hind legs, gripped the bars with hairy claws and began to dangerously shake the entire wagon. Chains and shackles around the beast's wrists and ankles thrashed and rattled. The beast opened a wolfish mouth and let out a terrifying howl. Heinrich, having made up his mind to have fun and not fear a circus act again, made his way forward. The crowd whispered to each other,

"It's so real. Look at that makeup."

"I wouldn't want to meet him on a dark night."

Heinrich was reminded of a man in shackles he'd met only hours ago, but he was sure that that man, Ivan, whose appearance had also been disturbing, was far more real than this creature. Suddenly, the beast howled again, slinging saliva from two-inch yellow fangs, and the crowd leaned back as though repelled by a force, and the ladies shrieked. Then, like a group of punching dolls, they all leaned forward again, as, before their very eyes, the beast transformed. It visibly lost hair and shrank until all that was left was a poor, exhausted man.

Heinrich took another step forward. *Impressive*, he thought. *Another clever illusion like the one in the gypsy's cabinet.* He looked for a trapdoor but the floorboards looked solid. The base of the wagon did not look especially thick, as might hide a wolf costume. He looked for mirrors or a hold in the roof of the wagon but found nothing out of the ordinary except the tired man on his knees with his hands and feet in what were now oversized shackles.

Interrupting his speculations, he became aware, in his peripheral vision, of an arm which jutted out next to him. Turning, he faced a man's shoulder which he followed to where it terminated in a finger pointing to the cage. The owner of the arm spoke,

"An incredible transmutation. A beast furiously fighting,
Is revealed to be a man, exhausted, afraid and hiding."

XVI The Wolfman

The speaker wore a gray suit, a full beard and a top hat which made his already impressive figure seem even taller. He gazed at the cage as patiently as one who is ready for anything to happen but doesn't need it to. Pinned above the man's front pocket was a golden brooch in the shape of a Hercules beetle, which intrigued Heinrich as he had just seen his first real one that morning. Also intriguing, the back of Heinrich's brain tickled with an uncanny sense that he'd heard the man's resonant voice before, but he couldn't place it.

"I'm still wondering where his costume went," Heinrich said. "I can't find any trap doors or mirrors."

The man did not immediately reply, but continued pointing.

"It looks like the performer could slip through the bars and be out of that cage now." Heinrich offered.

To this the man replied,

"That man is not in that jail for the usual reasons,
He will not harm others, and thus he requires no prison.
He is not a captive to hide away like the average troublemaker,
He's captured because he is running away, hiding from his nature.

That man is an escape artist, and there's an exit from that jail,
But he does not find it; for he escapes himself and ever fails.
He is fearful of his shames, he keeps them hidden away,
And he becomes a raging beast, to keep us all at bay."

"What do you mean? He can't get out?" Heinrich asked. The man lowered his arm and looked at Heinrich at last,

"He's trapped because his fear makes him become the beast.
Look, can you see the shackles securing his hands and feet?
As a man, they are too large for him, he can slip them and walk free,
But when he remembers he is ashamed, he returns to being the beast!"

It was as the tall man described. The man in the cage could easily slip his hands and feet from the shackles, yet he didn't do it. As Heinrich watched, the caged man seemed to notice the crowd for the first time, and shrunk away from them with a growl. Then, as sudden as his transformation from wolf to man, but in reverse, he began to grow in size and sprout hair, and his wrists and ankles grew into the restraints.

The tall man spoke again,

"In our shames we are not different, with secret burdens to bear,
We have them in common, our weaknesses are things we share.
This is not a magic act, magic is not escaping, it's accepting.
In that cage, I hope he learns the power of revealing and reflecting.

In a way, he may be lucky. If only we all could be so bound,
To expose our shame and fear until the chains fall to the ground.
Reveal your shames Heinrich; they are as common as they are small,
Don't fear to find that once exposed, they're not that great at all."

So finished the Great Mephisto as his austere facade cracked with a slight, warm smile.

Chapter VI
Ivan

He could not say how he knew, but Heinrich recognized who was facing him, and he was star struck. If anyone could be the hero from Able's stories, this was the man. The Great Mephisto gave a friendly motion for Heinrich to walk with him, which he was more than happy to do, and the two began to tour the grounds. Walking alongside the Great Mephisto, Heinrich found himself looking up at the man more often than at the circus around them. Despite being the leader and conductor of the whole spectacle, the Great Mephisto humbly blended amongst the crowd, unfazed by the occasional bump of a distracted gawker backing into him or the racing child running by his long legs. He looked content as he gazed over the heads of the crowds, and took in the sights along with them. *He must be proud*, Heinrich thought, *to see so many people enjoying his show.*

At a point where the thoroughfare turned to the left, the Great Mephisto dropped his chin, glanced at Heinrich, and then veered across the flow of people to the right and slipped into the shadows between two tents. Heinrich pardoned his way across the flow of humanity only to then dodge ropes and sandbags between the tents. On the other side, he emerged into an area at the back of the tents and stages where the noise of the crowd was faint. Supply crates and equipment stacked against the tents. A flap opened and a bald man rolled out a barrel of trash to the delight of several mangy cats. The man grabbed a box of chickens and disappeared back into the tent.

The Great Mephisto, seeing Heinrich arrive, resumed walking along a small path tread in the grass. Following the Great Mephisto, and no longer distracted by the action of the circus, Heinrich had a moment to think. The Great Mephisto had picked him from the crowd just like the falconess; and knew his name, like Leonora the gypsy. *There is a mystery here I am not getting*, he thought.

A gaggle of colorful showgirls flocking in a loose line around an old caravan interrupted his thoughts. They were adjusting each other's costumes, combing each other's hair, and chatting excitedly, while apparently waiting for something. A sign hanging above the caravan's door read, "Masquerade" in gold paint. At the steps of the caravan and the front of the line, with a brush in one hand and a tin of face paint in the other, stood Ivan. He was laughing with a dancer who held her face up to be painted with his brush. Heinrich was amazed to realize that Ivan, with his own face covered by scars, was the person in charge of makeup. Recalling his own shock when he had first met him, he noticed that some of the showgirls in the back of the line looked a bit apprehensive about approaching Ivan.

"I know the man doing the makeup," Heinrich whispered to the Great Mephisto. "I met him on a train here. I think some of those girls don't know him yet and may be a little shocked by his appearance."

The Great Mephisto responded,

"Then let them be. Do you consider Ivan to be deformed,
Or do you find it wonderful that he's so curiously adorned?

Those showgirls may have flawless faces, wrinkle free and smooth,
They bear not the profundity of life as his face shows every groove.
For each scar is a new lesson learned, each crack, a new experience,
Those hard lines reveal an extraordinary life, not a horrible appearance.

For someone to miss that, it would be their loss, not his,
Often what one sees distracts one from what really is.
The girls can gawk and point, he is not the one who cares,

When they see him unaffected, they will learn to stop their stares."

"Okay, fair enough," Heinrich said. "It's funny he doesn't use a little makeup himself, though."

Mephisto turned to him,

"Why should he, there is nothing wrong with what you see,
The only trouble out there may be what you perceive.

Ivan does not hide from truth, with that brush he is only brushing,
Inside his tin of miraculous makeup, there is absolutely nothing.
He brings out the real beauty of how people were designed,
He just brushes away the dirt, letting each performer shine.

He stands there unashamed and smiles, that is what he shares,
If he can accept his looks, then the ladies can accept theirs.
And look how they smile when he is done, you cannot disagree,
He is beautiful who does beautiful things; that is what there is to see!"

XVII Masquerade

Chapter VII
The Serenade

Ivan is truly nothing like he'd appeared, Heinrich learned for the second time and likened him to the harmless milk snake whose red and white stripes perfectly match the venomous coral snake. Appearances could be very misleading. As proof, he couldn't believe the showgirls had no makeup on, but it was hard to tell when they were all smiling, which makes anyone look good.

The blue sky had begun to warm in color and settle into afternoon. The Great Mephisto walked ahead again, beckoning for Heinrich to keep up, although the encouragement was unnecessary; Heinrich would have followed the man anywhere. They emerged from behind the tents and the Great Mephisto stopped, stepped aside, and extended his arm. The largest crowd yet was gathered around another exhibit. Apparently, this was the act the Great Mephisto had made the short cut behind the tents to arrive at. In a giant tank of water, protected by a gruff old sailor, a beautiful mermaid swam and waved to the crowd.

Heinrich smiled to see none other than the heroine of Able's wildest tale. She fit the legend perfectly. Her costume, including long red hair and an iridescent green tail, was remarkably real. *Did Ivan do her make-up—with real paint?* he wondered. The girl dove and made fish faces at the crowd from under the water, holding her breath for a miraculously long time. Heinrich held his breath and tried to match her, but exhaled a full three minutes before she surfaced again. When she spotted the Great Mephisto, she waved and smiled so brightly that Heinrich guessed the *'love'* part of Able's tale might be true. The look on Mephisto's face as

XVIII The Mermaid

he bowed to her in return confirmed it.

The Mermaid grabbed the rim of the tank and with a sweep of her tail, jumped up and perched herself on the edge. She wrung out her braids, flipped them over her shoulders and began to sing. Her first few notes were quiet and seemed to stray but as her volume rose, Heinrich winced and leaned back, and brought his hands to his ears. The girl's voice sounded like a coal car whining down the rails in a deep hollow mine. *That is not,* he thought, *what a mermaid is supposed to sound like.* Strangely, the Great Mephisto had closed his eyes and seemed to be enraptured.

"Is that singing?" Heinrich asked, nudging the Great Mephisto. "Does she think that's how a mermaid sounds?" He paused, embarrassed, realizing this was the love of this man's life he was talking about, and attempted a compliment, "Impressive courage though."

The Great Mephisto's eyes twinkled as he watched the Mermaid and said,

"A bird is made to fly; courage does not spread its wings,
That there is a mermaid, Heinrich, and a mermaid sings.

Have you ever heard a mermaid sing her song before?
It's like a waterfall crashing down upon a rocky shore.
It's a faraway noise, like that of an ocean squall,
It's not like any music we have ever heard at all.

Listen to her music, don't be concerned if it's good or bad,
She allows the unique and new, something we have never had.
She sings in her own way, in a way that's not been done,
For the simple reason that she loves to, and she's the only one.

To be herself is worth it, though she may stray a note or word,
No one knows how she should sing, so it's the greatest siren song they've ever heard.

Hear this message, Heinrich, when you listen to her song.
If something is worth doing, it is worth doing wrong!"

Truly the consummate showman, Heinrich thought. The Great Mephisto had not shown the slightest hesitation in asserting the girl to be a real, bonafide mermaid. The Mermaid's voice rose, bringing Heinrich's focus back to her, and teased the crescendo of her strange serenade. It was true that he'd never heard anything like it at all. He leaned forward and closed his eyes. The Mermaid's voice trembled, then reached a climax as raw as a field of cicadas trying to out-sing a forest of mockingbirds. Heinrich was swept up with inspiration. The Mermaid's voice was bold and unique, flawed and triumphant, breaking and tripping over itself only to rise stronger and prouder. At the very moment when the song began to soar, and Heinrich's heart swelled in his chest, it broke, stumbled and quivered for a moment, and lay still, quiet.

The mesmerized and appalled crowd stared as water sloshed against the sides of the tank and dripped in puddles on the ground. The songstress looked at the quiet faces, then raised her arms and beamed her most brilliant smile. A joyful shout and a tumult of cheers, applause, and whistles erupted. *So much for my first opinion,* Heinrich thought, pleased to have been wrong. Mephisto bowed again, this time a bow of deep respect and gratitude to the Mermaid, and began to stroll away. Heinrich waved to her, but she did not notice as she watched only the Great Mephisto. Heinrich caught up to him and admitted,

"Okay, I am impressed." Then he ventured a question he needed an answer to, "Tell me something. A man named Able told me a story. He said you and the *'mermaid'* met on a faraway island." Heinrich spread out his hands. *Did he have to actually ask?* He did anyway,

"Who makes up these stories?"

Mephisto looked at him with a sly smile.

"Then you have heard why my life is blessed and why I thrive,
And that the loving kiss of a mermaid will keep a man alive."

Heinrich burst out laughing. "Oh, come on!"

Mephisto face revealed amused contemplation rather than comedy. *Unbelievable,* Heinrich noted again. The man still stayed faithful to the promotion of his show: the girl remained a real mermaid. *Very well,* he thought. *It's just entertainment.* As Heinrich accepted this interpretation of the stories and experiences yet again, Mephisto stopped at the edge of a field. The shouts of the crowds had faded into the distance. A light breeze brushed the tips of pale wild rye as tiny flies and seeds floated above the grass and flashed in the sun. Beyond the field, a group of men drove stakes into the dirt while beyond them, other workers assembled a framework for stands that could seat hundreds. Mephisto raised an eyebrow and gave Heinrich a sidelong look, as though gauging him, and then spoke,

"Allow that I explain the truth, so all may be laid plain,
In this fantastic show, there is no truth constrained.
Everything is real; no actors nor costumes feigned,
These are real creatures, exposed and unashamed.

Every strange attraction I've assembled is sincere.
Real is the gypsy's trick; real is the Wolfman's fear.
I wanted a world where a mermaid could swim out openly,
Where anyone could shine, however they are made to be.

But there's not a single person in those crowds walking by,
Who chooses to see the reality right before their eyes.
One day I want to tell them all, so they may learn and grow,
But people are scared of change and things they do not know.

From acceptance of new ideas, so many folks refrain,
I believe that is the cause of so much worry and so much pain.
I wonder at the multitude of secrets that are kept,
Because folks are so unsure about what they will accept.

Every day I take a chance. Today I take a chance with you,
Wonder at this world, Heinrich; oh, how much you never knew."

A shiver ran through Heinrich. Goosebumps rose on his arms. *Imagine*, he thought for a moment. If everything was real it would mean a secret island—with a giant squid—did exist somewhere and that some men turn into wolf beasts and gypsies know the future. The vision in the gypsy's cabinet returned and chilled him like a cold breath on his neck. The scarlet curtain quivered in the back of his mind, threatening to expose the horrible mask that lay behind it. Heinrich's throat cramped and he swallowed hard. *Why does the man insist that I believe everything is real?* he demanded. *This is all just a show!*

He forced a smile.

"It may take me a moment to comprehend it all," he offered as sincerely as he could. He considered that maybe the Great Mephisto promoted the fantasy to encourage people's imaginations to let loose and enjoy. Heinrich decided he could try that, but still wondered why the Great Mephisto had selected him.

Chapter VIII
The Marionette

Heinrich found himself alone at the edge of the field and wondered how long he'd been lost in thought. Somehow the Great Mephisto had left him without his noticing or a goodbye, but he reasoned it was okay as the man had a circus to run. He, himself, considered finding a place to nap when a man approached and asked,

"What 'r ya doin' just standin' there? Give me a hand."

The man, who was holding one end of a piece of tarred lumber, jerked his chin towards the back end dragging on the ground.

"Oh, okay," Heinrich said without thinking. Forgetting his nap, he hefted the other end of the lumber, and the man, whose neck bent forward like that of a goose, led the way through the field toward the construction of the stands. Heinrich was glad the man was in front and couldn't see how he struggled to carry his end of the load. *Why didn't I just say I didn't work here?* he wondered.

As they approached the other workers, Heinrich could tell by the sweaty shirts and dirty faces that they'd been working in the sun all day, and he felt a little apprehensive about being late to the party. When they delivered the lumber, Heinrich asked the workman,

"What else can I help with?" The man extended his gooseneck over his shoulder, and said,

"Go find the man in charge; you'll know him when you see him. Master Tack's his name."

Heinrich nodded and looked in the direction indicated. Sure enough, standing out from the rest, a man with a chest as large as a barrel, was heaving a line with a heavy load. Heinrich approached though nervous about disturbing the big man, and asked,

"Master Tack?"

The large man ignored the question and Heinrich considered that maybe sweat had blocked his ears. Either that or now was not the time for introductions. Then Heinrich felt a sharp tug on his pants and a high-pitched voice cried out,

> *"Yes, what may I do for you? I'm a busy man you see,*
> *Nothing? Okay, let me show you what you can do for me."*

The speaker, apparently the real Master Tack, whose head came to just below Heinrich's knee, pointed his chin straight up, exposing a scrawny neck. His two small hands were poised smartly on his hips and his open face looked ready to help—if help could be asked for in a timely manner. While Heinrich struggled to reply, Master Tack jumped up and grabbed the rope from the barrel-chested man and pulled it down to a stake with ease despite the rope looking heavier than him. Heinrich, amazed, found it all the more difficult to offer an introduction, and Tack didn't bother to wait for it,

> *"Are you good with rigging, knots, tackle, blocks?*
> *We need a hand and we are racing against the clock!*
> *Follow me; see what needs be done,*
> *You can help while still we have the sun."*

The sprite-like man began to skip about the workers. Two men were pushing up a frame and Tack leapt above their heads and kicked the frame into place. A group of men were slugging hammers at a stake and Tack grabbed a sledgehammer and sank the stake with a single strike. All the while he sang to encourage his crew,

> *"Look up, it rises high,*

The sun is in the sky!
Be bold, reach that height,
Bust your back and use your might.
Feel the heat, sweat and burn,
Shine bright, watch the sun and learn!
Heave ho; heave high,
Work and don't ask why!
We have no time to lose,
We have just the time we use.
Use your brawn; rest your worried mind,
Move muscle; leave your thoughts behind.
Raise that support! Good God man, pull those strings,
If you don't, then let someone else do all these things!
Let the world see we love its wondrous plan,
We have work to do because we do all we can!"

Heinrich followed, thrilled by the vitality bursting from Master Tack, and astounded by his costume. He inspected Master Tack from every angle as he jumped around the construction site, and Master Tack seemed to be made entirely of wood and constructed like a small marionette; he even moved with a light careless trip in his step like one would do if supported by strings from above. Of course, there were no strings or anything else Heinrich could find to explain the phenomenon. He considered it possible that Master Tack could jump so high because he was so light, but then he could not account for the man's strength. Of all the costumes and impressive abilities Heinrich had seen that day, Tack's had him the most perplexed.

"You make it all look so easy," Heinrich observed. "You pulled twice the weight of the largest man." He reached out and tapped Tack's small shoulder. "What is this... costume? Is it wood?" He waved his hand through the air above Tack's head. "How do you work?" he asked, forgetting his resolve to stop worrying about how it all made sense.

XIX Master Tack

"You will not find strings or springs, or jumping bugs, my friend.
In fact, how I move is something I don't altogether understand.

The only account I can offer for my having a life and voice,
Is that I'm full of energy because there is no other choice.
Examine me for how I work, you'll not find a coil or key,
I work, not for what I am, but because I need to be.

Anyhow, it's clear I work; I should ask why you aren't yet,
You are flesh and bone, but you haven't broke a sweat!"

"Well," Heinrich replied, "I just got here, but I could work if I knew how." Tack threw up his little arms and said,

"Then what are you waiting for? There is no how,
The answer is very simple: do, and do it now!

You are a man with the gift of life, but you don't fight the fight.
You don't do all you can, and still, you think you might.
You should be as desperate, you should yearn as I yearn.
Show me what it is to live, that is how I learn!
Reveal the powers that can work through you, prove you are alive,
Life begets living and action, action; thrive and you will thrive!

When I see the industry of others, it inspires me to do.
Look! I started living because I desperately wanted to!
Some said I couldn't live because I am only glue and wood,
So I measure myself by what I do, not all the things I could!"

The little man's triumph became slightly more serious as he stepped closer to Heinrich, looked up, and said,

"Who am I to think I matter? That I should live . . . that I could dance?
That I could beat the odds? That I could win? I'll tell you who, I am!"

Heinrich felt like he had an inkling of what a miracle might look like and a tear fell down his cheek. The little man dashed off to encourage more men and kick more things into place. Heinrich wiped his face and let his reason return. Tack could not be a wooden doll, though Heinrich noted that imagining him to be, as he'd done for a moment, was fascinating and powerful. Tack's words stirred him, and as he had nothing else to do, he joined the men working and began to sweat in the afternoon heat. He focused on the lifting and hammering at hand, and his questions about the circus: why he had been singled out, and why the acts were never revealed, fell away from him like his sweat.

Three hours later, a grandstand stood assembled around a large oval arena. The next step in the construction was to lift the large tent that would cover the stands. Heinrich wondered why the crew hadn't put the tent up first and thereafter worked all day in the shade, and was told that the train carrying the tent had made some important detour and been delayed. The sun reached the horizon, and Heinrich now wondered if there was enough daylight left to loft the canvas, as it did not appear it would be an easy task. But just as he started to figure how it would even be accomplished if they had the time, Master Tack commanded everyone to make way.

Almost beyond comprehension, a twenty-foot tall man strode majestically into the arena. His pants and linen shirt were roughly stitched and matched the style of the other roustabouts but were of a size that probably required more cloth than all the other men's clothes combined. The Giant had big eyes, long black hair, and an angular face. He reached down and began lifting tent poles up like pencils and connecting them to the rigging and canvas. Upon raising the main tent pole, the rigging lifted out of the Giant's reach and even he was unable to make the final connection. Right before the sun set, Karl the Strong approached. He grabbed the Giant's foot, hefted it above his head, and the Giant was able to secure the final connection. Tack's small voice interrupted Heinrich's bewilderment. He held out his little hands to the great tent and said,

"This tent, like the world, will be filled with wonder, sights, and songs.
And amongst all that confusion it'll be hard to know where one belongs.
But don't try to fit in; there's no vacant place or empty role,
You must add. Reveal something; unearth an honest soul.

The reason you are here is to reveal what others haven't seen,
Brush away the dirt of expectations and shine what's never been.
Don't waste time deciding how you want to be defined,
Do and be aware as actions reveal your design.

Maintain a steady faith in this life you've been apportioned,
Because of, not despite your flaws, you are vitally important.
You have never happened before, let us see it all,
From a towering giant to me, the great and very small!"

XX The Giant

Chapter IX
The Giant

The great towering tent resembled Gulliver tied down by hundreds of little ropes as it darkened against the purple sky. The roustabouts, including the Giant, headed to a clearing behind some tents, where supper had been prepared. Heinrich followed the gang, spooned himself a bowl of garlic and potato soup, and sat down by the campfire.

The Giant settled on a sturdy crate and it creaked with the weight, threatening to collapse, as he slurped his soup from a wash tub. The soup dripped down his mustache onto his pants. Finished, he licked the tub clean, then wiped the soup from his pants and cleaned it off his fingers in the same way. Everyone else sat languidly on logs or lay stretched out in the dirt as they finished their meal. Unlike the hobo camp, there was little conversation. The men, hungry from a hard day's work, kept their mouths close to their bowls, shortening the distance their spoons had to travel, as they shoveled in the broth. Red embers dispersed against the backdrop of a thousand twinkling stars; tiny hints of the blazing behemoths beyond.

Heinrich tilted back his bowl, catching the last piece of potato on his tongue, and looked over at the soup pot. A few men stood in a line waiting to scoop out seconds. He decided it was too much of a hassle to get up and wait, and figured he hadn't worked as long as the others anyway, so he scooped out the last remnants of soup in his bowl with his finger and leaned back. Under heavy eyelids, he examined the wonder that now amazed him more than Master Tack, the Giant. The Giant's knees bent at Heinrich's head level and his ankles poked out of his ill-fitted pants at the level of Heinrich's knees. The Giant's thin nose and almond colored skin suggested he came from a race of men in the Far East. *Perhaps somewhere out there, men can really grow so tall,* Heinrich reckoned. The Giant's head loomed high in the shadow of the night; his train wheel sized eyes reflected the fire, so two fires appeared to burn in the sky. Master Tack's high voice piped out,

"Hey you up there looking glum in all your glory,
We have someone new. Tell him of your story."

The Giant looked down at Master Tack, the fire lighting his features from below, and smiled revealing a row of crooked, sharp, gleaming teeth. He turned his big head toward Heinrich and Heinrich found it impossible to look away. The Giant began to speak with a deep voice and thick accent,

"I am a giant from the distant north and I am the only one,
So if a giant ever did a thing, then it's something I have done.
I have been the only one forever, and I am very old,
I imagine after I was made, the Maker broke the mold.

If you feel insignificant in the great brotherhood of man,
You will find the idea of one of a kind, tough to understand.
So, I will tell you . . . it was tough! There was no one to show me the way,
And alas, there was no one to teach me, when I went astray.

No one opposed me, there were no regulations,
None had gone before me, I never learned of obligations.
I did not understand that helping others would, in turn, help me,
Instead, I pushed them all away, for fighting is very easy.

I would do as I pleased, and I was proud; I had it all,
Oh, I can remember it, I stood . . . I stood soooo tall!

And from my lofty height, I could never know,
What there is to learn when one is, at last, laid low.

Sometimes, unique and proud, I found myself alone,
And I resolved the only company I needed was my own.
At other times I was a marvel and was treated like a king,
And I could take what I wanted, so I wanted everything!

The more I received, the more I deserved, I was never satisfied,
And I laid it to waste without a care; such are the ways of pride."

The Giant lifted his eyes to the sky.

"Oh, they were great and opulent times, but now they only hurt,
For when I was at my very best, I was at my very worst.

The lands I knew became barren; they could not satiate my lusts.
And I exhausted all goodwill and shattered every trust,
And when the people knew me not for God but bane,
I would leave them wasted, proffering only my disdain.
And so the wells were emptied and became few and far between,
And I began to wander further to the places I had never been.

I journeyed to a cavernous valley, walled in by rugged mountains,
Where waterfalls gushed from the cliffs like so many frothing fountains.
I followed a river they fed and it led through a jungley land,
Where creatures hid in the trees making calls I couldn't understand.
I clambered through hanging vines and the roots of ancient trees,
Until I was arrested by a sound, sadly familiar to me.

So shocked and curious was I, I commenced an investigation,
And in a pit of deadly sinking sand, I made a revelation.
There trapped were seven tall women, in terrible distress,

XXI Campfire

So I plucked each one up from certain suffocating death."

The Giant uprooted a bush with his forefinger and thumb. He brought it up to his face and gazed at it cheerlessly while he resumed.

"This is how I met the warrior women, never before recorded,
How I came to be their hero and was subsequently rewarded,
How the princess was amongst those I'd saved from the fast thick mire,
How she recognized my worth and offered all I might require,
How they sought my protection, and hoped to keep me near,
For I can see in the dark and I can't conceive of fear.

And how I was proud and great, and how I showed what I could do,
Though not to be of service, but for the worship my deeds accrued."

And Heinrich had thought Able had an imagination! However, despite the absurdity of the tale, he was envisioning it all. Likely the Giant's being twenty feet tall was helping, as that absurdity was an undeniable fact. The Giant continued with a shake of his head,

"Working to impress grew tiresome, I came to resent my idolaters,
Before too long I realized that I did all their labor.

So, I flew into a rage that I should work or stress,
For, a strange thought comes with power: that to be great is to do less,
And that to be important in some twisted way should mean,
That one no longer has to do great or important things!

So I announced I would be king, waited on foot and hand,
To be succored and amused, to be the one to make demands.

Such is the madness pride can cause, such was my inverted reason,
The mighty maidens of the morass refused, and convicted me of treason!

XXII Quicksand

I protested they were wrong; I extolled my worth and left no virtue out,
But the more I preached, the deeper were sown the sneaking seeds of doubt.

And though I'd been a savior, and despite my impressive acts,
I was forced from the tribe by poisoned spears and axes in the back.
I fought like reckless thunder. How I fought! What a battle we had!
But the poison sapped my strength, as I was too greatly stabbed.

They drove me to the mountains, and I lost myself in snow,
But I minded it no longer, for I had no place left to go.
I shivered as I mused that I'd been the greatest in the land,
But alas, I had been the most greatly unwanted useful man.

And as I stood alone, I thought about my worth,
Everywhere I'd been, I'd become a scourge.
Tears became ice around me as I recalled these memories,
And the cold gnawed at my bones, as my flesh began to freeze.

There I spent a thousand years, in the extremes of land and weather,
Until something finally happened that started to put me back together.
The blazes of youth and pride smoldered and expired,
Time and suffering alone served to snuff those fires.

I say, one may try so many things to cool those fires down,
But only time and experience can bring a foolish man back around."

The Giant blinked, turned away from Heinrich and stared into the fire with an intense and searching gaze, as though the fire were speaking to him like a portal to the distant past. Slight snoring sawed around the fire. Only Heinrich and Tack still sat upright. Heinrich glanced up from the crackling fire. He'd been imagining what it would be like to be lost in the wild, frozen by regret. The Giant continued to look into the fire as he resumed in a hushed tone,

XXIII The Giant Battle

"Now the lesson from my tale is not what you may think,
Do not be meek and modest. Stand out on the very brink.
My lessons came from living wild, and they are my greatest wealth,
So I say go live wildly, find your lessons by yourself.

Do not play it safe, do not keep under control,
Go out and beat your chest, be wild, expose your naked soul!
Make trouble, make noise, live out loud, try to be intensely great,
Go to the greatest extremes, life will teach you how to moderate.

If I could do it over, as I often try to do in better dreams,
I know I would not; wisdom comes from going to the great extremes.
Wisdom does not come easy . . . It costs dear . . . It is a heavy, heavy price,
But pay it, my man . . . Pay that cost . . . That is my best advice!"

He clenched his giant hands into fists and looked again at Heinrich,

"I have suffered, it is true, perhaps my advice seems strange,
But regrets are just for those that do not learn and do not change.

And though I've learnt and changed, I will leave you with a thought:
Having no regrets doesn't mean there's a dire deed that I've forgot.
I still have a sadness, and I am forever haunted by this ghost . . .
Of all the pain, the pain I caused, is the pain that hurts the most!"

The Giant leaned forward and placed his head into his palms. A tremble shook his body and he was quiet, giving the stage to the crackling coals and crickets chirping in the brush. *He still struggles,* Heinrich mused and realized, true or fantasy, there was real emotion behind that story. He thought about how different his life was to the Giant's. He had never done anything extreme. Even after his father had died and left him that letter in which he had encouraged Heinrich to follow his heart, he had played it safe. *To be fair,* he thought, *I am not a giant.*

XXIV Imprisoned

The Giant let out a long, low sigh. He hauled his bulky frame up, his joints popping like the fire. He staggered, almost as if he would tilt over, saluted Master Tack, and strode into the open field where he could stretch out and sleep. The other roustabouts continued sleeping around the dwindling fire with their jackets pulled tight around their hunched shoulders and their hats lowered over their eyes. Heinrich felt his own eyelids getting heavy, and swiped aside some rocks in the dirt and laid down.

As he adjusted his arm under his head, Tack tapped him on the shoulder and beckoned him to follow. Beyond the sleeping men, Tack showed Heinrich an a-frame tent with a cot inside. Heinrich breathed a tired "thank you" and crawled in without a moment's hesitation. Before collapsing into the cot, however, he turned and whispered a question,

"Hey, how'd the Giant free himself from the ice?"

Tack laughed a joyous little laugh and answered,

"By the same grace that to us all has happened,
The Great Mephisto discovered him abandoned.

Then Mephisto made low the frozen walls of affliction,
That served as both the Giant's fortress and his prison.
He said, 'Hide not, this life is worth enjoying,
Your sad defenses are no more than annoying!'"

Tack left a lantern and a thoughtful Heinrich before skipping off into the night. Heinrich distractedly unlaced his boots. A layer of dirt caked his hands and black tar stuck under his fingernails like the coal used to do. *Have I hidden from enjoying my life? Should I have taken more chances?* he asked himself, too dreary to consider the answers. He found a small bucket of water, a wash towel, and a small mirror next to the cot. He picked up the mirror. After only a glance, he let the mirror crash to the ground where it shattered into pieces. Blood drained from his face and he gripped his throat. He lurched up, knocking over the tent, and tried to cry out, but only spurts of wheezing escaped. Fear and agony clutched at him and he bolted into the night.

Chapter X
Medina

Heinrich doubled over with exhaustion. He fell to his knees, his hands struck the grass, and he panted like a steaming train. He concentrated on his breath and it slowed down as the fear retreated. He began to take in his surroundings. He was between two larger tents softly lit by the pale green light of the moon. A cricket chirped and soon the others joined, convinced it was safe to sound out again. In the mirror, he had seen the same ghastly face that he'd witnessed in the gypsy's cabinet. He knew that was impossible and reasoned that he was just delirious and exhausted. He had heard too many fantastic stories throughout the day, and they had overstimulated his imagination. His tired mind had been tricked by the lantern light and had pictured the face from the gypsy's cabinet. He looked up at the full, smiling, faraway moon. *What the heck am I doing at a circus?* he thought. There had been nothing to fear in the plains. He should have never jumped that train. The stillness and dark of the fields beyond the circus beckoned; it would be easy to sneak away, and he decided to do so. However, Heinrich only made it a few paces when the quiet was fractured by several striking sounds.

Whatever that is I don't care, he thought. He disregarded the nonsense the Giant had said about taking chances, not having regrets, and whatever else. That was not who he was, who he had ever been, and it wasn't going to do him good now. He just needed to get away. The striking sounded again, closer. A faint light shined from the corner of a long tent, where the canvas had come untied. Heinrich hesitated, cursed his curiosity, and crept over and peeked in.

Grim paraphernalia crowded a candlelit interior. By the far wall, a metal casket with spikes on the inside of the lid stood next to a cage large enough to fit a person. A rack with straps and buckles lay against wooden stocks designed for the wrists and neck. Axes, spears, and swords were stuck in the ground, and glinted with reflections of the flickering candle flames. Shields, battle hammers, and devices Heinrich would not even hazard to guess the purpose of leaned against the wall of the tent. The clutter of cutlery surrounded a narrow aisle in the center of the tent. At one end of the aisle stood a tall wooden target covered with gouges, the vast majority in a tight circle in the center. Thirty feet opposite the target stood a statuesque woman with alabaster skin, ink-black hair, and a fist full of knives. Her long legs, encased in striped stockings, sprouted from a short ruffled dress and terminated in small leather boots. The lady thrust forward and with rapid flicks of her hand, she let loose a series of flashing blades toward the target. They all struck home in the dead center.

Whether or not the torture devices were mere circus props, this performer's skill was very real, and very deadly. Heinrich decided he had seen enough and that now would be a good time to leave. He inched backward when suddenly a splitting crack jolted the tent pole in front of him and a blade appeared quivering in it. The woman now glared at the opening in the tent as she called,

"Come out! Come out creeper, spying in the shade.
I never trust the secret ones, hiding and afraid.
I know what lurks in doubt, only trouble, only terror,
Come out or taste the blade, my knife is never thrown in error.

Blessed is he that fears the dark and in it what lies hidden,
And cursed is he, who hides amongst those dark shadows forbidden,
Who are you that wishes to be concealed in the night,
Are you afraid to be exposed? Afraid to be brought into the light?"

Heinrich cowered to the side of the opening. He could not run faster than the woman's knives could fly. He cursed himself for not leaving when he'd had the chance, and not having a better option now, he parted the tent and cautiously stepped inside. The lady ran her fingertips along the edge of a blade as she watched him enter. Heinrich kept one eye on her as he looked around the tent at the collection of cruel equipment. In a corner to his right, a tall dark shape sat on a crate, reminding him of when he first noticed Ivan in the corner of the boxcar. The shape appeared to be a mannequin wearing a suit of armor and adorned with a scarlet cape. Its glimmering bronze breastplate was molded to resemble musculature. A rust stained helmet with slits for the eyes, nose and mouth, encased the entire head and neck. Heinrich was just about to look back at the lady when a dark speck appeared on the mannequin's leg. It seemed to have dropped from the helmet. Heinrich noticed that from the eye slits, dark rivulets of some substance ran down the cheeks onto the iron collar. Nearest the eyes it ran ruby red. Very slowly, as in a nightmare too horrifying to be real, the iron-clad head turned to face him.

Heinrich screamed and jumped backward, knocking over a spear and looking for the exit. He looked at the woman, now the lesser of two evils.

"I'm sorry for looking in," he stuttered. "I couldn't sleep. I heard a noise. I only looked..."

To his surprise, the tall lady laughed and put her knives down on a chair.

"It's okay, now that I can see you, you've no need to be scared,
Not of me or of my cloaked companion over there.
My name is Medina, we are performers in this show,
I am not that bad, and despite his appearance, he is far less so.

Accept my apology; I'm on edge, leery of the lurkers,
I had no idea you were just one of the workers.
I have a keen sense of danger and I sense something in the night,
It is not you I guess, but something does not feel right."

XXV Medina

They are just performers. It's a show, Heinrich reminded himself. Medina's voice and laugh soothed him. His heartbeat eased from its pounding and he felt safe from fainting—for now.

"What do you sense?" he asked, "I think I may sense something too. A terrible vision seems to have started haunting me since I've come to this circus." He couldn't believe he was admitting this.

Medina cocked her head and focused,

"What? Not only my heightened senses perceive a danger,
Tell me, what are these visions you have seen, dear stranger?"

"I don't really know," Heinrich replied, "It is a faded, yellow, twisted face with rotting teeth."

"No!" Medina gasped.

A brief, vulnerable fear betrayed her confident facade. She gripped her shoulders and began pacing and mumbling to herself. She kicked the dirt with her boot and said,

"Then it is true, the wicked one comes, he looks like what you say.
Why he comes to you I cannot know. You need to run away!"

Medina looked up and began to explain herself,

"When I was young, I was in love; life was fresh and full of promise,
I would wed my darling Victor, who was brilliant, kind and honest.
But his parents would not have it, so we decided to elope,
Trusting love to guide us with hearts full of faith and hope.

Our fortunes were not great, so with the little we could manage,
We planned to board a vessel and work the deck for passage.
But the fair sex is seldom welcomed, so we devised a plan,
We should be like brothers, myself costumed as a man.

XXVI An Elopement

On the docks, we met an eager captain assembling a crew,
He seemed as willing to have us work as we were willing to.
Oh, I should have seen the signs! For every time he breathed,
I saw he had a foul mouth and out dropped rotting teeth.

Alas, once at sea, the nature of our work was clear,
We were in the company of pirates and forced to volunteer.
My darling Victor balked at this, but I fretted and I pleaded,
I could not afford to be discovered, and for my sake, he conceded.

But he did not join as I did . . . I hesitated not, I will confess,
I became an asset to the crew, one of the captain's best.
Though I began fair and gentle, I feared to reveal I was a maid,
So I turned dark and terrible; I learned to throw the blade."

She bowed her head and wrung her hands as if debating whether it would be more painful to go on or to stop. Her hard exterior softened and Heinrich caught a glimpse of the innocent girl Medina must have been before boarding the pirate ship. He wondered if it was because she had been so innocent that she now carried herself so dangerously, or if it was due to the trials she'd endured. *Life can be cruel,* he thought before he caught himself getting swept up in another tall tale. The captain she'd described fit the description of the pirate in Able's stories. Heinrich was amazed by what a good actress Medina was, and didn't want to ruin her story, but he had to let on that he had heard a similar one.

"Do you know the story of the Great Mephisto?" he asked.

Medina nodded her head and told,

"Aye, Mephisto suffered the same captain, long before my shame,
Though his vessel was wrecked at sea, Rabar remained unclaimed.
I fear Rabar is still alive, and his hatred still persists.
The only hope I hold is that he knows not that we exist.

XXVII Pirates

And I pray he knows not that Mephisto was likewise saved,
For the last time I saw Rabar, he sent me to a watery grave."

She looked up with misty eyes and Heinrich thought she might stop there, but Medina went on like a sinner with a penance to serve.

"In battle, I was a banshee, and it served as a distraction,
No one noticed that Victor avoided cruel and violent actions.
This did not last, however, for one fatal day, a victim caught,
Rabar ordered that I should dispatch the prisoner with a shot.

And I was to do it! I would do it! I tell you I prepared to pull the trigger!
But my Victor would allow no more. He roared, 'I beg you, reconsider!'
Then to the shock of the crew and myself, he cut the prisoner's ties,
He said, 'Let us play by your twisted code, who say, "Eye for an eye!"

'Be it mine instead of his, that you put your bullet through,
Let him live, and end my suffering what's become of you.
'Do it! I'd rather be blinded; lift me from this curse,
To go on seeing how you lie, is for me a fate far worse.'

Rabar, bearing witness roared, 'Do not disobey or orders give,
Do you really think I want to trade your life for his?
'You want tit for tat? Oh, that you would be so bloody wise . . .
Very well,' and to me, he told, 'shoot out one of each their eyes!'

Victor looked at me and said, 'I could not have you for a wife,
I cannot accept that you should think to take another's life.'
Hearing this, Rabar roared again, 'You take a man to be your wife?
I have not heard, in this wretched world, a stranger thing in all my life!'

'You foolish devil!' Victor returned, 'Look at what you've done,
For your cruelty, see what my maiden bride has now become!'

I realized how far I'd fallen, how deeply I had failed love,
Fear had made my choices, fear had shaped who I'd become.

Oh! I'd let fear trample love! I let loose my long black hair,
So I became, for one last moment, who I'd been when I was fair."

Medina looked up, and trembling, finished her tale,

"As cowards and deceivers, we trod the plank with both hands bound,
Weights secured about our feet to ensure we both would drown,
Rabar howled as we fell, 'I know your faces and your names,
Now fathom this before you die! You should always be ashamed!'"

Medina's voice faltered. A tear finally spilled, leading a deluge down her cheeks. Heinrich was bewildered that she had survived and moved at the same time. He tried to comfort her by saying,

"But you are here. You survived."

Dark makeup streaked Medina's pale face. She nodded and said,

> *"I am just a hollow shell of who I was, but yes, I did not drown,*
> *How, I will not tell you, but I washed ashore and I was found.*
> *No, it was not life my sins deprived me of,*
> *I lost a treasure far more precious, I lost my love."*

A convulsion overtook Medina and she began to crumple inward like a paper doll. Heinrich wanted to help her, but he feared to touch her. The Masked Man's armor creaked as he rose protectively. Medina wiped her nose with her gloved hand and motioned him to stay. She held herself up and a pathetic grimace distorted her face.

> *"I am sorry, it haunts me still, I cry for the pain of all I've lost,*
> *But I was blessed, I once knew love, and that was worth the steepest cost."*

She sniffled one last time before her jaw flexed, her mouth tightened, and a fury ignited in her eyes. Her delicate brow dropped low and her voice rose,

> *"In place of love, I have a heightened sense of any threat,*
> *This is how I throw the blades, and how I'm not harmed yet.*
> *I wondered why I felt evil when just you were at the tent,*
> *But now I guess it's due to the vision you've experienced.*
>
> *It must be Rabar. Somehow we both can sense him coming,*
> *If I were you, poor roustabout, I would take off running!*
> *You've confirmed it, now I'm certain, take heed, this is your warning,*
> *It's the show he will lay low, so be gone from here by morning!*
>
> *I know a thing Heinrich, a thing I hope you'll never feel,*

XXVIII The Plank

I know the loss of a life stolen! There are some wounds that never heal.
He comes tomorrow, I can sense it. Then the hard times will begin,
So run unless you want to be here when the great storm crashes in!"

Chapter XI
Heinrich's Dilemma

The Masked Man rose and stepped closer to the agitated Medina. She again held out a halting hand. The man acquiesced, but gestured Heinrich to leave. Heinrich nodded and immediately backed out of the tent. One does not defy a man with blood coming from the eyes of a mask over his head.

Back in the safety of the night, Heinrich's heartbeat finally returned to normal. *You heard her, run!* he thought. *Could it all be true?* As wild as Medina's story had been, it had explained a lot and matched with the other stories he'd heard. Additionally, she had trembled with genuine fear just as the Giant had been genuinely remorseful. As for his own vision, be it Rabar's face or just his imagination personifying a sense of dread, it was a very unsettling mystery that had definitely only started at the circus. It was time to be rid of it all.

He snuck through the grounds until he could see the prairie's expanse spread just beyond a final row of tents and wagons. The grass swayed in the warm breeze, rising and falling as though breathing, and glowed with the light of the moon. As he passed the last caravan, a hunched shape stepped into his path. Heinrich nearly jumped out of his skin but remained rooted in place. The figure held a lantern up to its face. It was Leonora, and her one good eye glared at him. She croaked,

> *"Leaving so soon? Looking pale and white,*
> *Why do you go sneaking around in the dead of night?"*

The gypsy was the last person he wanted to see.

"I don't belong here!" he whispered, "Wasn't that in your crystal ball?"

The gypsy only tilted her head.

"Get out of my way. I don't need this!" Heinrich insisted and tried to brush past her, but Leonora stepped in his way again and hissed,

> *"Do you know what you need? You sound uncertain,*
> *Tell me, what did you see behind the scarlet curtain?"*

Heinrich stopped as though he'd just hit barbed wire. Leonora had sounded curious, as if she didn't know. *This is too much*, he thought, *she is playing some twisted game.*

"Your foolish mask you frighten people with," he said.

Leonora countered,

> *"You've seen it once more, haven't you? The way you tremble it's made plain,*
> *The blood is draining from your face; you've seen the vision once again!*
> *You've already guessed the truth my boy; a shade is becoming clear,*
> *Behind the curtain is just a glass, it's time you face your fears!"*

"Move hag! I don't care about your riddles!" Heinrich shoved Leonora aside, and startled by his own fierceness and all that had made him fierce, he began running. The gypsy called after him, piercing the quietude of the night,

> *"Whatever you have seen, it's not me that made it so,*
> *It's not a gypsy trick, it's something you refuse to know.*
> *If what you've seen and heard cause you doubt and dread,*
> *Consider what about yourself you doubt and fear instead!*
>
> *Don't run now, Heinrich! Don't run away and hide,*
> *Sometimes the greatest discoveries are when we look inside.*
> *Accept this place and all the questions, accept the defects of your own,*

XXIX A Warning

Learn what there is to learn between the fire and the roughest stone!"

Leave me alone! Heinrich pleaded silently, but above the sound of his fleeing, her shriek stabbed at his eardrums again,

"Yes, the dark storm is coming! I have seen it in the ball,
But if you run to where you risk nothing, you will risk it all!
Whatever you have done or whatever you've been through,
The only thing that matters now is what you are going to do!

You are running from your demons, you hide them in the shadows,
You run to the plains again, where life is empty and action shallow.
Come back lost soul! Come back Great Gift, there is wonder to be found!
Come back and hone your metal! Shine upon these testing grounds!"

ACT THREE
The Show

Chapter I
The Fantastic Strange

Morning broke over the circus grounds to find every tent raised, each string of lights strung, every flag atop its pole, and bundles of colorful balloons dotting the sky like floating gumballs. Performers made the finishing touches to costumes and makeup, organized their props, and took their places at booths and stages.

The entire town had heard the reviews from those that had visited the previous day and was now gathered at the front entrance. They huddled like freshly ironed heaps of coats and scarves steaming on a cold day, as they speculated about what to expect. The conjectures turned to gossip, which gave way to murmurings, which rose to nervous chatter, and then a silence bloomed; they still had no idea.

Then someone hushed the crowd and they all whispered for the rest to be silent. Fifty yards away, a man appeared perched on a camel. He steered the camel up the thoroughfare toward the crowd, and as he proceeded, performers stepped from tents that lined either side of his path. There was a turbaned man with a tiger on a leash, a short-haired woman with a python draped over her shoulders, a man with a long, white mask made of bark who held a torch, a thin man with a grass skirt who had a bone through his nostrils, a muscular woman crowned with a Viking helm, and a clown on a giant bicycle. At the front entrance, the rider surveyed the crowd, then he extended a hooked staff. He bowed and as he sat up again, he raised a rope barrier with his staff and motioned for the people to enter. Then he tugged the camel's reigns and loped back down the thoroughfare.

The people streamed into the grounds like the morning light breaking through the summer fog and spread out to explore any direction that caught their interest—every direction. At each turn, barkers promised sights to awe, amuse, and delight, and with the large and exotic animals, contortionists, dancers, and daredevil stunts, none were disappointed. Along with acts and stages, there were tents that offered viewing collections of paraphernalia from the unknown lands: shrunken heads and tribal masks; tapestries depicting turbaned crowds worshipping blue gods with multiple limbs; a ship model six feet in length, with tiny cannons that actually fired; tanks of ferocious fish that could glow in the dark; and the skeleton of a half man, half alligator. Musical acts included a barbershop quartet, two opera singers, and a man operating a calliope tooting out throaty, playful tunes from a wagon. Adding to the cacophony, gasps and shouts filled the morning as the crowds discovered each surprise.

At exactly noon, a few visitors noticed the entrance to the large bigtop in the center of the grounds was open. They entered, found seats in the stands, and took a break in the shade. Though the air inside was static, it was much cooler than outside in the sun. A diffused orange light filtered through the taut canvas roof revealing painted designs like Indian doorways decorating the high walls. In the top of each doorway design, a giant Egyptian eye of Ra, painted in blue, stared down at the arena. Two forty-foot tent poles soared from the arena and pushed the roof towards the sky. Rope ladders led up the two poles to two platforms which were connected by a high wire.

Soon more people trickled into the tent and consequently, the crowds outside gradually became thinner. When the people outside began to wonder where everyone had gone, they began to ask questions. Soon everyone shuffled in and found a seat until the entire population of the town packed the stands. The collection of people, many of whom only knew of each other and had never really met, found themselves randomly arranged. The fancy, dressed in linens, sat amongst the more modest, in patches and second-hand clothes. Families sat next to lonely people who were sure the children were not being raised right. The quiet and the shy sat between the loud and the laughing; the successful met the dejected; the dreamers saw the steady; the lucky ones bumped shoulders with the unhappy ones; lost people found people with purpose; all in no particular order, but with one thing in common: they were there to see a show.

Once the shuffling in the seats died down, the people became expectant. They looked around, wondering if they had all made a big mistake, as there had never been an announcement of a show in the tent. All the same, the universal sense was that so large an error would not have been made and even if it had, some commencement should take place regardless, because there they were. When still there was nothing but silence, the murmurs of uncertainty began.

A boy sitting far in the back heard the crunch of gravel and noticed a man lift the side of the tent and creep in. The man wore a long grimy coat and his full beard was parted so that it pointed in two directions.

Heinrich would have recognized the hobo from camp, but he had run away in the night. The boy looked around to see if anyone else noticed the dusty wanderer as he stumbled towards the center of the arena. When the others did see him, the murmurs hushed. Certain that he was not part of the show, the crowd became both disappointed and anxious for the lost hobo, but they remained seated and waited for someone else to help him. When he reached the center of the arena, he looked up and jumped as though shocked to find himself surrounded by so many people. His face, however, expressed no great surprise. Slowly, he bowed low and standing up straighter than anyone expected, he pointed at the ceiling of the tent. With a tremulous voice, he called,

"Rent up there, is a tear in the tent!"

The entire crowd looked upwards in unison. Sure enough, a small beam of light was shooting through a tear in the high roof of the tent. Suddenly, a fluttering shape interrupted the beam. It stopped briefly and the culprit, a bright orange butterfly, climbed into the tent. The hobo called,

"From that tear, from that crack, from that imperfection,
Enters something beautiful, a reminder from the heavens!"

The butterfly floated down the sunbeam and landed on the hobo's outstretched finger. Everyone followed this flight and beheld the man with his two-pointed beard, now bathed in light and miraculously changed as though by some magic. His ragged clothes were gone and he now wore a white costume fitted with a cape and a tall turban. He seemed taller and radiant, his eyes were full of life, but his clothes and demeanor were not the only astonishing difference: hundreds of butterflies now perched, fluttering their wings, along his outstretched arms. The audience gasped. The man turned carefully in place and announced,

XXX The Great Mephisto

"Welcome, everyone! Now we begin the show!
Be prepared to wonder, forget everything you know.
This is the show of astounding truth so all will be made plain,
*I am the Great Mephisto! Welcome to **The Fantastic Strange!"***

You have one task today, whatever you experience,
You must trust it all and take joy in your existence!"

He raised his arms sharply and the host of butterflies exploded in a colorful chaos of flight like a field of flowers sweeping up in a tornado. Horns blared outside the tent, followed by a marching band that streamed through a performer's entrance in full stride and bluster, their brass horns flashing and sounding. The snare drummers kept a rousing rhythm accented by beats on bass drums so large they bent their bearers' backs. Following the uniformed musicians of the band, the calliope wagon entered piping out its funny tunes. The calliope rolled near the center as the band spread to the perimeter. Dancers tumbled into the arena, followed by a charge of juggling clowns who seemed to be able to juggle their own projectiles and also those of their fellow fools, tossing them to each other across the arena. Flipping acrobats and trapeze artists appeared swinging out from the high platforms. The Great Mephisto, glowing in the center of the action, held his arms straight out and continued turning in place. At last, when the tent seemed near to bursting with dancing, color and sound, he dropped his arms and the action slowed. The music quieted and the performers filtered out of the entrance as abruptly as they'd come in, and now accompanied by the butterflies flying above their heads. The band did not leave the tent but squeezed into a cordoned off area in the stands, and like that, the introductory festivities had appeared and gone in what seemed only a brilliant flash. The Great Mephisto followed the last performer to the exit, but he did not leave. When the flap of the exit fell shut, he turned, stood to the side, and announced,

XXXI The Cavewoman

"Ladies and Gentlemen, for our first act, we go back in time,
To the very distant beginnings of man and woman kind.
I present to you a relic, one of your great ancestors,
She will go wild! Behold the formidable Beast Master!"

The curtains blasted open as a lion and a saber-toothed tiger charged into the arena with the Bearded Lady balanced on their backs, one foot on each, and looking as ferocious as both. Her pink dress and parasol had been exchanged for an ensemble of hyena skin and a lion tooth necklace. Her beard looked barbaric and her hair flowed behind her like a billowing cape. The audience leaned back against the knees of the folks behind them as the savage trio raced around the arena roaring. The people eased back in their seats as it dawned on them that if anyone could control such dangerous beasts, this wild woman could. As though to prove it, she jumped the animals through large rings ablaze with fire.

Chapter II
Heinrich's Second Dilemma

Heinrich awoke groggy, as though a dense cloud filled his head. He rolled over and shut his eyes tighter against the blinding red of the sun through his eyelids. His face felt hot and the earth beneath him felt warm and soft. The crisp scent of dew-damp grass filled his nostrils as he listened to the trickle of water and the rustling of grass. *Had he passed out here?* He shaded his eyes and massaged his head. Wisps of a nightmare rose into his mind like steam.

He sat up to pull the pot of dreams off the fire of unconsciousness. Rubbing sleep from his eyes, he looked at pink sweet pea flowers opening for the day. He pushed his hands in the dirt and stood. The breeze chilled his chest; he'd been sweating. A song sparrow called from somewhere behind him. Gray hairstreak and eastern tailed-blue butterflies fluttered over the wild rye. The hills in the distance were a warm purple, and before them was only plains and the occasional tree, all around.

The nightmare drifted across his mind again and left a lingering impression of pirates, a gypsy, and a woman wielding knives, mixed with the sense of a wolf-man, a mermaid, a giant, and a marionette. *Incredible,* he thought and shook his head.

He shuffled over to the stream, kicked off his boots and rolled up his pants. The cool stream soothed his feet. He splashed water on his face and looked into the shadow he cast on the surface of the stream. Dirty water drops dripped from his chin, disrupting the surface. The ripples settled and an image began to take shape. A face stared back at him from the shallows of the stream. Heinrich choked, his throat went as dry as dust and he tried to cough. The face drew him in, he could not move his neck. The desperation of claustrophobia closed in. He was trapped in his own body. He tried to scream but it found no escape and only pressured his insides. The face rushed at him, yelling as it charged face first into his face. Water closed around his head and his scream exploded from his mouth in a jet of bubbles. He reared out of the water gasping for air and stumbled to the sandy bank. He dropped to his knees and whispered,

"Why me? Why is something haunting me?"

With wet, muddy hands he pulled the small envelope from his jacket pocket. *Heinrich* was written on the front in his father's hand. He removed the note, and though his hands trembled, he read the words he knew by heart. Words that had haunted him for thirteen years.

"Take this small fortune, and use it as you need,
Find your path, follow your heart where it may lead.
I saw it in you when you were born, I see it in everything,
You, my son, are great; you will do great things."

He'd scrawled over the first two lines with a pencil years ago because he didn't have the small fortune anymore. A sum his father had spent his life saving. It had just sort of trickled away. Rent and taxes rose, his salary never did. Things needed fixing, but he didn't have time, so he paid someone. New clothes, a meal out every once in a while, a good cause, books he meant to read, subscriptions he never cancelled to travel magazines he just threw away—it had all added up somehow.

Water dripped from his hair and made the ink on his father's note run. He crumpled it in his fist and wondered if he was going crazy. He whispered aloud,

"I'm glad you never saw what I became. I am not great, and now I'm going mad. Don't look down. Please don't look down now."

High above the plains, amongst whispery clouds, a falcon looked down and saw a lone man get up from a stream bed. The man laced his boots and then ran in the direction of a small circus five miles away. The falcon changed its course and, at last, it headed home.

Chapter III
The Butterfly

Thunderous applause erupted for the Bearded Lady/Beast Master as she rode her big cats out of the tent. She returned on foot, opening the tent flaps with both arms high, and the appreciation surged again. The Bearded Lady curtsied and walked to a place along the edge of the arena to watch the next performance. All the while she also scanned the faces of the crowd as though searching for someone. The Great Mephisto approached the performer's entrance again and called out,

"I have traveled to the farthest reaches of every land,
And in one of the great extremes, with pick and torch in hand,
I discovered our next performer frozen in the ice,
So I chipped away his prison and brought him out alive.

Behold a man who is very different, and see that he is awesome,
And then be amazed to realize how much you have in common!"

A thump sounded outside, followed by a slight tremor through the stands. After ducking low to fit through the entrance, the Giant crept into the tent, and upon reaching the center of the arena, expanded to full height. His head almost reached the acrobat platforms. A brown leather winter coat lined with white fur flowed from his neck down to his shins; a regal bronze helmet capped his head. Shouts of surprise were stifled by disbelief as the audience leaned back and looked up.

XXXII Winter In A Tent

The Giant flashed his toothy smile and displayed in his hands two wooden controls made of cart axles lashed together, which he began to manipulate with fingers surprisingly nimble for their size. The controls operated several strings which hung down and were fastened to Master Tack's arms and legs, completing the perfect semblance of a marionette dancing at the ankles of the Giant. Six cellos and a violin from the band began a slow melody and the Giant started to dance. He strode around the arena, his coat sweeping behind him, as he appeared to control Master Tack, who held out his arms and jumped like an ice skater. The Giant twirled near a side of the arena, shaking the tent poles and stands with each step, and swung Master Tack like a flying sprite over the heads of the crowd. The Giant concentrated on keeping Master Tack from striking any of the astonished people as he watched his own feet to ensure they did not smash into the stands. Tack, on the other hand, laughed as he flew so fast and close to the faces of the crowd.

Tack reached into his little pockets and flung handfuls of glitter in a shower behind him like that of a shooting star. From the platforms high up the poles, silhouetted against the bright ceiling of the tent, puffs of what looked like dust swept into the air. As it drifted down, it was seen to be snow which coated the audience like powdered sugar, melted quickly and brought a welcome cool to the tent. The massive Giant swayed with the drift of the snowflakes and the music of the cellos as Tack flew through the flakes letting them splash against him.

At the side of the arena, the Great Mephisto watched enthralled, though he must have seen the act one hundred times, and held out his hand to catch the snow. Then someone entered the tent behind him and before he could look, he was jerked sideways. To his shock, Heinrich clutched at his arm, breathing heavily, with bloodshot eyes and sweat pouring down his face. Heinrich opened his mouth to say something but only wheezed. The Great Mephisto leaned closer but Heinrich only wheezed again, released his grip and collapsed. The Great Mephisto knelt and quietly gathered him in his arms and carried him from the tent without disrupting the show. Across the circus grounds, he entered his own tent and propped Heinrich in a rickety chair. He grabbed a cup of cold water and poured a gulp in Heinrich's mouth. Heinrich coughed, his eyes snapped open, and he looked frantically from side to side.

"Mephisto," he gasped between breaths, "Help me. I cannot escape it . . . I am haunted. It followed me. A vision. Make it go away."

The Great Mephisto brought his hand to his chin and rubbed his jaw before replying,

> *"You see some sort of specter, and robbed me from my show,*
> *Why is this my concern, and if so, where would I make it go?"*

"I don't know, but it all started here with the gypsy." Heinrich said desperately, "Medina thinks it's Rabar, the pirate in the stories. I don't know what to believe. She thinks it has something to do with today's show. I know it's crazy, but maybe it's a warning... something dangerous is coming."

The Great Mephisto handed the water glass to Heinrich. Neither the news nor name of the pirate seemed to ruffle him in the slightest. He asked,

> *"If what you say is real, what would you have me do?*
> *I told you this was real. Should I run away like you?"*

"No!" Heinrich gasped, figuring the gypsy must have told him that he'd run away. "It followed me. It can't be escaped. You have to believe me. If any of this is true, something terrible will happen!"

Mephisto replied,

> *"If a dark presence approaches to destroy all I have made,*
> *Should I hide or should I tremble, how should I be afraid?*
> *If tragedy awaits me, what preparations should I make?*
> *And tell me, how can I know this is a fate I should escape?"*

Heinrich deflated in disbelief. The Great Mephisto would not break his mystical character.

"I don't know, but help me escape it at least," he appealed. "I cannot handle things like this."

The Great Mephisto pointed to a corner of his tent and for the first time Heinrich noticed dozens of cages stacked on each other, standing on ornate pedestals, and hanging from the roof. Inside the cages, hundreds of butterflies fluttered and opened like colorful flowers. Heinrich had never seen so many butterflies before in his life. Mephisto held out his hand and a single butterfly flew from a cage and alit on his outstretched finger.

"How can you be so calm?" asked Heinrich, "What if something really does happen? To the circus, to the people?"

The Great Mephisto blinked as slowly as the butterfly wings opened and closed, and said,

> *"Perhaps it's time it did,*
> *Tell me, do you know what this is?"*

He held out the butterfly and Heinrich raised his hands in surrender. "Yes," he uttered. He recognized the black and tan marbling decorating the butterfly's dusty wings. "It's a hackberry butterfly."

Mephisto raised an eyebrow at this intelligence and nodded,

> *"Caterpillars have no idea that one day they'll have wings,*
> *They don't compare what they are to what the future brings,*
> *They don't curse their shape or fear how life might turn out,*
> *They do not run from fate or fight to bring their change about.*
>
> *For the caterpillar, it is simple, there is one guarantee,*
> *If it stays alive, it becomes what it was made to be."*

If it stays alive, Heinrich thought, recalling the butterfly that had

XXXIII The Show Goes On

died in its chrysalis when he was a boy. *That butterfly will be dead in a week tops anyway,* he thought. *What was the point? Why not just stay a caterpillar? Why risk it? Why does anyone have to be something?* The butterfly flew from Mephisto's finger and he dropped his hand. His voice lowered to a tone more serious,

> *"Your perspective, just like mine, can never see it all,*
> *Do not fire your fears at me like some deadly cannonball.*
> *You demand to tell me what to fear, is it really so defined?*
> *Do you know what must be done? I need not be so confined!*

> *Maybe there is something here for you to understand,*
> *There are things you can't control, so give up your demands.*
> *I do not chase trouble, and I do not from it run,*
> *I'm aware it's part of life, and I allow life's will be done.*

> *Let hardships be a trial, not something you reject,*
> *Find in them a truth, find how much you will accept.*
> *The reason I am great is because I am a broken man!*
> *I pity those who believe their fears can be outran.*

> *I am great! Not because I fight or the forces I defeat,*
> *My greatness is measured by how I thrive when I am weak.*
> *I will bear witness to what happens, be I faint or be I strong,*
> *I will not judge what I cannot know. This show must go on!"*

The Great Mephisto bowed, then rushed out of the tent. Heinrich's head pounded. He reached for more water and watched the hackberry flutter around the tent. A breeze blew through the tent, twirling the butterfly like a piece of paper. He walked to the door of the tent. The hills looked so far away, but even out there he knew the vision had not left him. He recalled Medina who had told him the hard times would begin, but he felt weak. *I cannot run any longer. I give up,* he accepted. *What do I have to*

XXXIV A Siren Song

lose? Why not just be here when the great storm crashes in? He stood, dusted off his pants, and headed in the direction of the bigtop.

Inside the great tent, the Mermaid's tank stood in the center of the arena, surrounded by tropical palms in large pale Egyptian vases, A spotlight shone on the tank, casting swimming turquoise reflections around the tent like an aqua chandelier, making the entire audience appear to be seated under an ocean's surface. Iridescent bubbles floated down from the high platforms, popping on the crowd and surrounding the tank. Above the tank, with her tail swishing in the water, the Mermaid swung back and forth on a trapeze and finished her curious song. The final note echoed in the silence of a mesmerized crowd. The Mermaid blew a kiss, spread out her arms, and cheers erupted at once. The Great Mephisto had arrived in time to see it, standing just inside the entrance as he gazed at his love. Heinrich snuck in quietly and was relieved to see that nothing terrible had happened, yet he couldn't shake a gnawing anxiousness.

At the edge of the circus, a dark figure also listened to the Mermaid's final song. He inhaled through a crooked nose and exhaled a foul breath. He spat a tooth onto the dirt and made his way past empty tents, vacated stages and abandoned caravans. Just outside the bigtop he grabbed a line and began to climb, fist over fist, his legs hooked over the rope, like one well practiced in the skill of climbing ropes to tall places. Applause and cheers reverberated the canvas walls. He muttered to himself,

> *"After all these years, the cruel coward remains alive,*
> *Filling people with foolish filth and ruining foolish lives.*
> *Was that music? How disgusting; how the empty masses cheer,*
> *Entertained and distracted by what they should reject and fear.*
>
> *There are ways to act and behave, ways this coward is resisting,*
> *One's worth must be proved, not measured in the joy one has existing."*

Chapter IV
Medina's Act

Circus hands rolled the Mermaid's tank to the side of the arena, next to the Giant, Tack, and the Bearded Lady, so she could watch the rest of the show alongside them. She noticed the Great Mephisto had returned, and leaning over the edge of the tank, she waved and gave him a questioning look; he'd missed making her introduction. Mephisto bowed deeply to her with the sincerest regret, then strode to the center of the arena. Heinrich stepped under the stands and leaned against the scaffolding.

In the spotlight, the Great Mephisto closed his eyes and folded his hands on his chest. The audience hushed. Then he stretched his arms out and pointed at a tall wooden board with a painted target of concentric circles, which had been placed near the center of the arena, and at the performer's entrance at the opposite end of the arena. In a serious tone, he commanded,

"Please now all, your quietude and your discretion,
You are not the only ones who will have to pay attention.
The next performer must have all her wits intact,
And all her concentration during her terribly perilous act.

This is a show of courage and skill, I bid you hold your breath,
As we witness the next performer attempt to defy her death.
Though she is dark and mysterious, be you not afraid,
Welcome for your suspense, Medina, Mistress of the Blade!"

A loud thud echoed from the target where a blade now trembled in the center of the bulls-eye, glinting in the spotlight. From the direction the knife had come, the performer's entrance, Medina appeared. Her black hair was piled high on her head and a corset and layered tail skirt fitted her lean figure. She focused on the target and walked into the arena, though she seemed to falter a step as though sensing something when she passed Heinrich in the shadows of the stands. As she strode towards the target, her right arm jolted with blinding speed, hurling three more blades across the arena. Sparks flew as the blades crashed into the first and sunk into the very same crack in the target.

The tent opened again and the Masked Man entered, following Medina and carrying a large woven basket in his powerful arms. Thin trickles of blood dripped from the eye slits in his helmet. Heinrich stepped further into the shadows of the bleachers as the Masked Man passed him. A piece of popcorn dropped onto his head. The audience shifted in their seats uneasily but otherwise remained profoundly silent.

Medina pried the blades from the target with a practiced flick and turned to face the crowd with her chin held high and her skill proven. Silence. Medina's face was as expressionless as the Masked Man's mask as she gestured to two leather bindings bolted to the target. She stood in front of the bindings and spread out her arms, allowing the Masked Man to secure the bindings around her chest and feet. He gave a demonstrative tug on the leather belts, tightening the buckles and proving that Medina was strapped in. Grabbing the edge of the target, he tilted it back until it lay like a table with Medina facing the roof of the tent. He then drew six large knives from his belt and held them, shining above his head as he walked around Medina. He stopped, and with a flourish, placed three knives in each of her hands, bowed his iron encased head and retreated.

The audience held their breath. They leaned forward and did not so much as blink as Medina's arms thrust out like two catapults, sending the six knives shooting up into the air. Spinning and flickering like deadly stars in the heights of the tent, the knives reached their arc and came

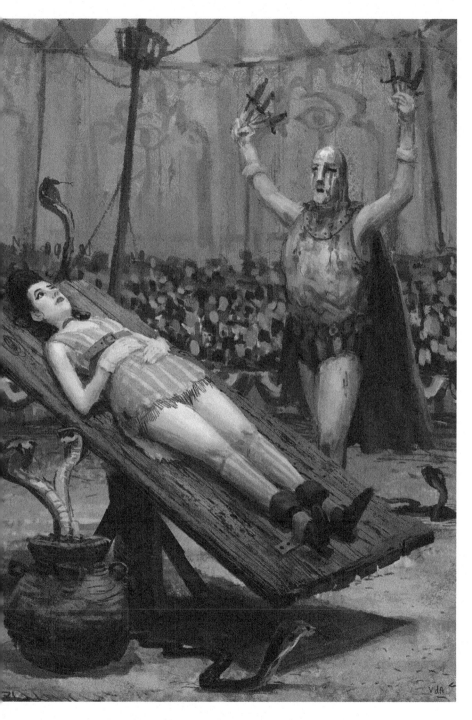

XXXV The Gamble

plummeting back down to from whence they came. They struck with the staccato of a firing squad. The blades quivered in the wood inches from Medina's body. The Masked Man approached and tilted the target back upright to reveal Medina outlined by the blades and unharmed. A palpable relief spread through the audience, followed by a timid smattering of applause.

Medina accepted the cautious admiration with a slight confident nod. Turning to the Masked Man, she moved her head to get his attention. The Masked Man stepped close and she whispered,

> *"Look I have missed!*
> *Nothing deadly, but I don't like this!"*

She flicked her eyes to the side. One blade had landed close enough to her neck to sever a lock of her black hair.

"This omen is clear, the wicked one is here."

The Masked Man nodded, bringing his bloody metal mask close to her white powdered face, and whispered,

"I shall keep you safe from harm.
Fear not. This show goes on."

Medina looked into the dark eyeholes of his mask, closed her own eyes and nodded. The Masked Man lowered her back down to face the roof and turned to the crowd. He lifted the large woven basket he'd brought, high above his head, and walked another dramatic circle around Medina. He set the basket back down and opened the lid to reveal a nest of vipers slithering and writhing over one another in a tangle of scales and tails. He reached amongst the serpents with his gloved hand and withdrew twelve silver blades. His voice resonated deep and hollow from within his mask, sending a chill through the audience,

"It is one thing to twirl knives and avoid a little cut.
But it is quite another to use blades poisoned in the viper pot.
To dodge the first round of knives is just a dainty step,
To dodge the blades of venom, this is a dance with death!

For your entertainment, watch a game that you should never play,
The gamble where, if you should lose, you must give your life away!"

Silence reigned once more. The Masked Man placed the blades in Medina's hands and retreated.

Outside, the dark climber reached the end of the rope thirty feet in the air, grabbed the top of a tent pole and swung onto the roof of the big-top. His long coat flapped behind him. His feet made faint depressions in the taut canvas as he surveyed the expanse of attractions and exhibits spread out below. A lion roared from its cage, but there was not a soul in sight. The tent beneath him rumbled with life. Towards the center of the roof, the flap of a small tear shook in the breeze. The man crawled over, conscious not to put all of his weight on his high-heeled boots, and peered inside. What he saw caused him to bring his fist to his mouth and bite down on his knuckles, stifling a roar. He recognized the woman who lay outstretched on a large wooden table directly beneath him. He hissed,

> *"How can this be, she lives? But how fitting she's at this place,*
> *The fool boy would let liars live, he would welcome her disgrace.*
> *And let her think that she could change, that she could be recast,*
> *But no, she must pay for her evil sins, pay the debt of a wicked past!"*

At that moment the woman thrust her arms towards the roof in a rapid succession. Her projectiles became clear as they rose closer to the man looking in. Twelve poisoned blades slowed, reaching their height, and turned point down with a flash. Inspired, the man drew a black dagger from his belt. When the twelve blades began their acceleration downward, the man sneered and let his weapon drop through the tear. He snarled,

> *"Poor lady, suffer no longer, here's a second chance to die,*
> *I am doing you a favor, you shouldn't have to live your lie."*

The extra dagger went unnoticed by the audience who watched the twelve blades fall back down. They heard twelve sharp strikes of the blades sinking successfully into the target and Medina lifted her head and wiggled her fingers to show herself unharmed. The audience rose from their seats as the Masked Man, his arms raised encouraging the applause, approached to raise the target. Then he stopped as a sickening thirteenth thud sounded. It was Medina's head falling back against the board. The Masked Man swirled. Dark blood, almost black against her pale chest, spread into Medina's corset. A black dagger was sunk, up to its hilt, through her heart.

The audience gasped and clutched at themselves and tried to cover their eyes. The Masked Man moved quick as a flash. He threw his cape over his wounded mistress and jerked loose her bonds. He gathered her up in his arms and rushed towards the exit. Heinrich ducked back into the shadows beneath the bleachers as the hulking metal encased man charged past him. Medina's head hung back on a limp neck, tears streamed down her cheeks, and Heinrich heard the Masked Man pleading,

"Do not die; remain alive, you must remain alive!"

A tooth fell from the roof of the tent.

The Masked Man laid Medina down on a patch of grass outside. Her breathing stilled. A bank of dark gray clouds began to cover the clear blue sky. A bloody tear dripped from his mask and splattered on Medina's shoulder. He wiped at it, only smearing the mess, and another dark tear splattered her neck. He stood and stepped back from the lifeless body and looked up. He swung his fists up striking either side of his metal mask. His knuckles crunched as the metal rang. He beat his fists against the iron again. He struck again. He held out his hands. A hollow moan interrupted by sputtering breath escaped his mask. Blood and spittle dripped from the mouth slit. He struck with his fists, the mask, again.

Chapter V
Judgment

The Giant, Master Tack, the Mermaid and the Bearded Lady looked expectantly at the Great Mephisto. He stood along the side of the arena as if frozen still. Heinrich clutched the scaffolding, holding himself up, and looked back and forth between the empty arena and the exit.

Suddenly, a blood-curdling yell broke the silent confusion. Everyone looked up and witnessed the point of a sword slash open the small tear in the roof of the tent. The sky was growing dark with the approach of a thunderstorm. A bundle of rope dropped through the opening, un-coiling as it fell. A dark figure in a long coat appeared outside the hole he had sliced open and yelled again as he gripped the rope and swung into the tent whilst brandishing a jagged sword. He landed in the center of the arena with a cloud of dust. Grime covered his coat and tricorne hat. Crusty, matted hair and a thinning beard dangled from his sickly green face. His yellow eyes behind loose, red-rimmed eyelids surveyed the tent.

This cannot be real, Heinrich thought. *Surely this is an act. It's just a show. Medina cannot be dead!* Furthermore, he realized, if this pirate was Rabar, it was not Rabar's face that haunted him. The pirate began to walk around and looking at the audience, he spoke with a harsh voice,

> *"Settle back fair people, I am not the one to fear,*
> *I have just delivered you from one of the evils here.*
> *Do you know who walked this stage, twirling throwing knives?*
> *A wicked lying woman who caused the man she loved to die.*

XXXVI Rabar

Yet she performed before you, as though she were forgiven.
And unaware, with your children there, you sat before the villain!"

A boom of thunder shook the tent as the storm arrived.

"All around me I see treachery, and so it makes me wonder.
How can you not know the truth? What is this spell you're under?
Are you blind or do you refuse the truth before your eyes?
How can you not realize the disguises of your demise?"

The pirate pointed to the Giant crouching on the side of the arena.

"Let's start from the beginning why don't we, we can make a list,
Of the dangers at this show, all the details you've ignored or missed!"
There, the most obvious, truly, an elephant in the room,
I have heard of a Giant from the north. This is he, I must presume!"

The pirate raised his sword and pointed to the Giant.

"Like the dancer he pretends to be, he's in a strange position,
Pretending he never killed an exotic tribe of wild women!"

The Giant stood up, towering over his accuser, but forgot he was
holding the controls attached to Master Tack. As he stepped towards
the spotlight, Master Tack tried to hide by swinging himself behind
the Giant's legs, but the pirate spied the little wooden man and roared,

"What's this?! What is this?! Oh ho, not just a giant troll,
Is that a voodoo doll? Does it move without a soul?"

The pirate leapt into the air and slashed with his sword the lines that
suspended Master Tack. Master Tack tumbled to the ground and held
still. The pirate landed with a somersault, leapt again and stabbed his

XXXVII Stabbed

sword into Tack's wooden chest, then lifted him up. Tack yelped and looked about wildly, flailing his arms and twisting his legs in attempts to dislodge his body from the sword. The Giant, who could smite the pirate with a flick of his finger, reached down to help his dear little friend instead, but the pirate raised Tack between the Giant and himself, and yelled,

> *"Stay back giant or I shall hack it into sticks,*
> *I'll carve him into something useful, perhaps a box of picks!"*

He shook his sword, causing Tack's limbs to rattle. The Giant stepped back horrified and the pirate continued,

> *"Look, people, this moving doll is not made of flesh and bone,*
> *What sorcery or black magic has made this toy its home?*
> *What unholy possession animates this block of wood,*
> *That it should cry, that it should dance? Oh, that it thinks it could!*
>
> *I know it is hard to fathom, but see it try to get away,*
> *Here before you acting, a thing not made of living clay!*
>
> *Witness all, take heed, that I've pierced a demon with my blade,*
> *That I will banish this haunted evil, so you need not be afraid,*
> *That I will destroy this stranger, I will dismantle this weird creature.*
> *That it should never have been allowed to threaten the people in this theatre!"*

The crowd watched in horror as the wooden man's terrified face looked around of its own accord without any strings operating it.

"Make it stop!" They murmured. Their concern grew louder. "Make that thing stop moving!"

Tack heard the cries of repulsion grow as fear spread through the crowd. Made to understand he was truly alive, the people wanted him to die. Doubt entered his mind and a spark escaped his little body. His head lolled to the side. The tent grew darker as the storm covered the sky.

The pirate flung the defeated, limp marionette from his sword, and pointed the blade at the Giant again,

"Now people, do you understand the evils I reveal?
What you thought was entertaining is also very real.
This giant standing two stories tall is no illusion,
He could tear down these walls and bring all of us to ruin!"

The Giant looked at the crowd, and like Tack, saw the people's expressions quickly changing. They cowered away from him, huddling against one another as they watched him distrustfully. Tears welled in his eyes as he saw that he again made people afraid.

With the Giant thus distracted, the pirate rushed in and thrust his sword into the Giant's foot. At the same time, a bolt of lightning cracked outside, illuminating the Giant who, blinded by the flash and by the pain, howled and lashed out his arms striking a tent pole. The pole snapped like a twig and the top half plummeted towards the stands, stretching the roof and snapping lines. The poles at the sides of the tent bowed inward. The Giant reeled back with a look of disbelief, stunned and mistrusting his unwieldy body to do anything to stop the disaster. Then the falling pole became tangled and jerked to a halt like a body at the end of a hanging rope, swinging perilously above the people's heads. The Giant stepped backward toward the center of the arena, appalled by what he had done, and crouched low and moaned,

"Oh no, no no."

The pirate, on the other hand, was exultant as he called to the crowd,

"He is not a puppeteer on stilts, playing with a dolly,
Look how he bleeds, he's real! Understand your folly,
Witness the destruction he has wrought, and know that is his least,

Yet the Great Mephisto has allowed that you sit beneath this beast!"

He turned to the Giant and shouted,

"Who did you think you could become, you will always bear the scars,
It's time you face the truth you brute. Be ashamed of what you are!"

The Giant looked at the destruction he had caused and at the intim-
idated audience again. He saw a woman shaking in fear and he grieved,

"What have I done? He's right. May I never again cause pain,
Oh, for all this time, I have not learned, I have not changed!"

The Giant ducked low and hurried from the tent, leaving the lifeless Master Tack in the dirt. As the tent flap swung back in place, the pirate introduced himself,

"Call me Rabar the captain, your savior from these strangers.
None of you were the wiser; you could not have known the dangers.
You did not in your wildest fears, believe it could be true,
That the Great Mephisto would bring a real barbarian to you!"

Rabar bowed, sweeping his long coat aside with all the grace of a crippled debutante. Dirt fell from his hat as his head tilted forward. The spotlight became the only source of illumination as the storm shadowed the tent. Rabar flourished a yellow, wrinkled hand trailing a sleeve of decrepit lace.

"Fair people, to see you all exposed fills my bones with rage!
So I will vanquish all these threats, and spit upon their graves.
Let this be the last act that comes to play this stage.
Be it I who ends this farce. Be it I who turns the final page!"

Chapter VI
The Storm

Heinrich crouched under the stands and watched between the shoes and shoulders of the audience as Rabar gloated. Heinrich's position behind the crowd, and the fear swelling in him brought him back to when he was seventeen. He remembered pressing through the throng of people outside the mine. He'd already guessed the truth, that his Dad was one of the men trapped in the collapsed tunnel. Harris was in front of the crowd answering questions with that miserable look on his face. He was explaining that a team was assessing if they could safely get to the men. *What do you mean 'if' you can get to them?* Heinrich had wanted to yell. *You have to do something! He can't die, I'm not ready for this!*

Rabar's shouting brought Heinrich back to the frightening present. He looked over at the Great Mephisto whom he expected would step in, but the man continued to stand as still as a frightened deer. *Do something*, Heinrich silently urged. *Do something!*

Rabar, spotting his next victim, approached the Bearded Lady. Mary put her hands in front of her face and turned away. With a disgusted sneer, Rabar grabbed her beard, twisting her neck, and began to drag her towards the center of the arena. Mary tried to stay on her feet, clawing at his hand to release her, but she tripped and her legs scraped in the dirt. Rabar tightened his grip and jerked her forward. In the spotlight again, he held her like a wild animal and shouted,

> *"Another real one, not an actor. Not a deranged disguise,*
> *Truly a bizarre Bearded Lady, just as advertised.*

She is not one of our ancestors, long ago deceased,
And she is not the hunter . . . She is the beast!
She is an abomination, something that should not be,
A confusing mix up of nature, is she a he or he a she?"

Rabar yanked Mary's head backward, facing it directly at the spot-light. She pried at Rabar's fingers and said softly to herself,

"No, this cannot be the end, I've not found him yet
I must see him before I die, don't let me fail my quest."

Though tears of pain streamed down her face, and she shook with fright, Mary called out to the tent,

"My name is Mary Haggard. Ulysses, why have you abandoned me?
I did not deserve this. Come back! Oh please just show me mercy!"

Rabar looked surprised by Mary's outburst, then leaned close to her and whispered,

"You gross and ugly freak, this is what you deserve.
How dare you believe that you have any worth?
Except perhaps if you were hunted for your hide,
And mounted as the freak you are, with the rest of you cast aside!

How dare you demand someone to give you mercy,
I will do as life has done: I judge you unworthy!"

Mary looked into Rabar's eyes and then closed her own. She hung her head defeated and looked not like a wild determined woman but a sad old man. Rabar pushed her violently into the dirt. Exhausted and spent, she crawled to the side of the arena where she stayed, shivering and uncertain like the beggar she had once been.

Outside, the storm darkened and winds swept over the circus grounds knocking over booths and sweeping up tents. The flaps of the bigtop exit whipped inward and a cold gust blew against Heinrich's neck and he remembered the day the mine collapsed again. *Why must life be so cruel!* He looked out the exit of the tent where the grounds had become dark as night. He didn't want to get caught out in the storm, but he desperately wanted to escape the terrors in the tent that seemed to trigger his saddest memories. As he debated what to do, the townsfolk murmured, sharing his realization that they were held captive to a morbid show by a thunderstorm.

The spotlight gave a grotesque definition to Rabar's features. Another tooth fell from his gray lips. He turned to the last performer remaining at the side of the arena, the Mermaid. He strutted in front of the tank like a ringmaster and said,

"And now fine people, now I'm sure you've finally guessed,
That is not a costumed damsel who holds her foul breath.
What tales have you heard from the men who sail the seas,
Of pretty, swimming sirens who lure men to shame and misery?

She is real, the stories true. Why, she once had my ship attacked,
And every one of my crew was drowned as this submariner laughed!
But, if there is any doubt, I'll prove it with this simple test:
Let her live without that water, and if not, may she lay to rest."

Rabar drew a pistol from his coat and aimed it at the tank. The Mermaid swam to the far side, for she had nowhere else to go, and looked desperately at her love.

The Great Mephisto's eyes stared, red and unblinking, but he did not immediately react despite the threat and the signs of destruction all around him. Medina's target stood empty in the shadows. Tack lay broken in the dirt. The Giant had run away. The Bearded Lady trembled in misery and defeat. Heinrich cowered beneath the bleachers afraid.

At last, the Great Mephisto stepped from the edge of the arena. As he came forth, he brought with him no signs of his suffering. He looked calm and determined, not defeated, and in a resonating voice he called a tremulous call that made the crowd jump in their seats, and it stirred hope within them.

"Terrible suffering once cursed my life when I did not expect it,
I thought I did not deserve misfortune, so I did not accept it!
As if I could pick and choose between happiness and strife,
But no! I deserve it all! That is what it means to live a life!"

The Great Mephisto began to pace. Rabar smiled cruelly and followed him with his gaze, while keeping the pistol aimed at the Mermaid's tank. The Great Mephisto continued,

"I was lost at sea and dying; my spirit weak and worn,
And all alone, breathing salted air, I recalled when I was born.
A forsaken babe left for the tide, I was found and I was saved,
So I became the babe again, though it might send me to the grave.

I stopped fearing what might happen, I let go control.
I stopped my demands, as I'd had none so long ago.
I lay humbled in the face of life, I let my will resign,
I said, 'Show it all to me, I will have an open mind.'"

He cast a long shadow in the center of the arena.

"And this is what the world gave to me, the blessings of a life so cursed:
Patience, kindness and appreciation, when I thought it had done its worst!"

Suddenly, the Great Mephisto looked to the right, straight into the crowd. His eyes glistened as his look pierced between the shoulders of the people and stabbed into Heinrich. Heinrich's knees began to shake. The Great Mephisto's eyes became like black voids and his look stirred Heinrich's sad memories to the surface again. *I did not deserve to have my father die!* he thought. *I will always suffer that loss!*

The Great Mephisto broke his stare, leaving Heinrich sweating, and spoke again, his voice rising in intensity,

"I accept the troubles that shall come; I'll not try to defeat them,
You will understand the man I am when you see my struggles and how
I greet them.
As the darkness approaches, I am here, ready to meet it,
To understand and to accept it, so I need not defeat it.

When the hard times come, and everything is demanded,
You will survive if you realize, you too are empty-handed.
Sometimes your rescue does not come from what you've got,
It comes from the strength you find because you have it not."

The Great Mephisto's red eyes returned to Heinrich and searched his soul. Heinrich looked away. The Great Mephisto bowed his head and whispered,

"I've made it so it is all laid plain,
These are the testing grounds, the place of so much wonder and so much pain."

Chapter VII
So Much Pain

The audience gripped the edges of their seats as the Great Mephisto walked over to the Mermaid's tank and stood between it and Rabar's pistol. He called to Rabar, as he once did on a ship being torn apart by a sea monster,

> *"Before you came, the sun shone and everything was bright and clear.*
> *Joy and appreciation flourished; there were no dangers here.*
> *No one was deceived; everyone was free to choose what they perceived,*
> *Their reality was the truth that they alone chose to believe.*
>
> *I brought this company together for I am like the sun,*
> *I shine on people for who they are, not for what they've done.*
> *I had faith, given the stage, their spirits would be shining,*
> *And I was right, it was wonderful, their quality was blinding!"*

He faced the crowd.

> *"I had faith you would enjoy it, so I welcomed all of you,*
> *I said take joy in your existence, that is all you had to do!"*

He gestured back to Rabar with both hands,

> *"But you, you come like this terrible storm and block out the light!*
> *You only see people for what they've done, not for what they might.*

And in your hazy darkness, where everything looks frightening,
You proclaim to wield the truth like a jagged bolt of lightning.

And your hate explodes like thunder upon all that you expose,
But you do not see the other side, the side you refuse to know!
Your viewpoint is selfish, but life should not be seen that way,
Refuse to choose, and let it show you, see all sides on display.

Allow things to be revealed, can't you see you're out of touch,
Destroy the convictions you've defined that make you judge."

The Great Mephisto finished and stood silent. Rabar, as he had done so long ago, rejected what the Great Mephisto said and he merely shrugged his shoulders, cocked his pistol, and adjusted his aim from the Mermaid's tank to the Great Mephisto's chest. The Great Mephisto lifted his chin and began to walk away from the tank as he continued,

"I do not fault you, wicked one, I welcome your imperfections,
Even though you reject yourself because you cannot accept them.

Now, if ever there was a time, release that vain need to control,
What is wrong or right. Take care before you judge your soul.
Or soon, I warn, if you have your way, you'll find a dreadful fate,
You will see the jagged void that follows in the wake of hate!

So I say to you, stop fighting! Or do my words fall flat?
Stop strangling yourself, your twisted tongue, unravel that!
Or do you think you can break me like you once tried to do?
Look! The cracks you made in me are where my soul shines through!"

The Great Mephisto raised his arms and his white costume actually appeared to grow brighter. He now stood opposite the Mermaid's tank, and as Rabar's aim had followed, she was no longer threatened, for now.

The Great Mephisto went on,

> *"You may not understand this now, and will do what you deem you must,*
> *But I pray one day you understand, all your judgments are unjust!"*

The Great Mephisto stood tall and locked his gaze with Rabar's. Rabar shuddered for a brief moment before his composure returned, and to everyone's horror, he drew forth a second pistol and targeted the Mermaid's tank once more. A cry came from the crowd and the Great Mephisto started forward, faltering. The Mermaid ducked under the water and pushed into a corner of the tank. Rabar spat out a tooth and roared,

> *"Enough folly! The Great Mephisto! The worst of all this lot,*
> *The champion of man? Oh, how much you have forgot!*
> *Don't you recall that day when I caught a thief aboard the ship,*
> *And I ordered he be stripped, bound to the mast and whipped.*
>
> *And a pathetic boy who'd become distracted from his chores,*
> *Cried for me to stop, and that insolent voice was yours!*
> *You told me the thief was hungry, as if that excused the sin,*
> *But I stepped aside offering you the chance to pardon him.*
> *That you stand bare and receive the lashings, only ten were to be his,*
> *Or not, avoid the punishment, but then you must the lashings give!*
>
> *I declare that it surprised me, how quickly you worked it out,*
> *And to this day I still hear that poor robber wail and shout,*
> *And I hear your crying as you tried to place the blame,*
> *And I see his back in bloody shreds, to be forever maimed.*
> *And it was I who snatched the whip from your shaking hand,*
> *I had not lost count and you had not stopped at ten!"*

The audience gasped so deeply it seemed they might suck the air out of the tent. The wind outside whipped the walls; ropes securing them buzzed with the strain. The Great Mephisto closed his eyes and dropped slowly to his knees as though heavily burdened. Rabar's voice surged with the triumph,

> *"He promises hope; he believes people can be redeemed.*
> *But not if he has to suffer, remember, it was I who intervened!*
> *Life is cruel and made him cruel, he should be controlled,*
> *Charlatan! He neglected to expose the nature of his soul!*
>
> *His life is one big sham! Behold a liar to beat the devil,*
> *And now he exposes the lives of your poor families to peril!*
> *Perhaps it's because he's an orphan, castaway without a name,*
> *With no one to teach him better. He should be **ashamed!**"*

Drool dripped from the sides of Rabar's mouth. He eyed along the sights of both his weapons, lowering the one on his right to aim at the kneeling Mephisto. The Great Mephisto looked up and opened his eyes again. He had an incredible look of perfect peace, not like a man defeated at all. He raised his arms in front of him with his palms out as an offering. He spoke and his voice swept over the tent like a host of spirits.

> *"The story is true, and many more sins I own,*
> *Let me never again hide my secrets, let it all be known!*
> *I celebrate who I've been, am, will be, let it be made plain!*
> *I am the champion of man, and I accept The Fantastic Str . . ."*

An explosion from each gun barrel cut him short. The Great Mephisto's body went limp and he fell face down in the dirt like a sack of potatoes and bled. The Mermaid's tank shattered, the water poured to the ground, sweeping the Mermaid out with it. She looked across the arena to where the Great Mephisto lay unconscious and tears poured from her eyes. She hacked, choking on the air, and collapsed in the mud.

The audience was so shocked they could not react. They made no sound as they witnessed the horror. The spotlight flickered eerily above them. Hope of any salvation died in Heinrich's heart. Death surrounded him as it had when his father died. *Why me?* he wondered. Looking at the Great Mephisto bleeding on the ground, he thought, *it is too cruel and you were wrong! Sometimes the show does not go on.*

XXXVIII All Is Ruin

Chapter VIII
The Masked Man

The combined explosion of the two shots echoed across the circus grounds. When the sounds reached the Masked Man, who had been weathering the storm beside Medina's body, he stopped beating his fists against his helmet. Like a man possessed, he slowly turned and began to march through the mud. The wind and rain pelted his iron chest and drenched cape. The blood from his mask mixed with the rain and spread like veins over his armor. He marched straight through the tent flaps and into the dense silence inside the bigtop. Every head turned toward him. Steam rose from his shoulders as he scanned the arena. His gaze traveled over the crowd, the Mermaid and Rabar without pause, but when it discovered the Great Mephisto's body, the Masked Man stiffened. Heinrich trembled underneath the stands with a feeling that the Masked Man may, in fact, be even more fearsome than Rabar.

The Masked Man walked straight to the fallen body of the Great Mephisto and Rabar only watched. The Masked Man hung his head and slowly shook it side to side. He raised his arms, palms up, and let out a mournful cry that resounded through the tent. He bowed his head again, then wailed at the unconscious body,

"I trusted you! I trusted you! Look at me, I have survived!
You told me one thing mattered. You told me I must 'remain alive!'"

He knelt in the Great Mephisto's blood, roughly gripped his shoulders and lifted his limp form up as though willing him to listen.

"And I did that, despite my sins, despite what I had done,
I did that because you judged not and said I could live on!
I endured you see! Even though I hid inside this metal trap.
I remained alive! **But you . . . you did not do that!"**

The audience, their shock finally giving way to grief, began to weep
as the Masked Man's misery echoed so well their own. Heinrich sym-
pathized on several levels with the Masked Man as his echoing moans
continued,

"How can you go? That is against your rules, tell me, how can you die?
If even you let evil win, then who, oh who am I?

I am so sorry, without your faith, and despite what you have shown,
I will not accept this horror! I can't survive here on my own.
I was only able to accept myself because you believed I could,
But is this what has come of it, the death of what is good?

You never asked why I wore this mask, or why my eyes bleed red.
You did not care what I had done, 'It is what you'll do,' you said.
You did not care if I was damaged; you said not to be ashamed,
You accepted me though you knew not my face, knew not my name.

You told me I need not hide. Now I'll do as you once asked,
I will show you who I am, I'll show you who I am without this mask!"

He tenderly lay the Great Mephisto's body back down, pushed up on his hands, and rose heavily to his feet. He faced Rabar and boomed,

"You are a wicked man, but you know not a thing of shame,
But you will understand it now. Know my face and know my name!"

The Masked Man removed the solid iron trapping from his head, and letting the mask crash to the ground, he held his bared face high. When his features were revealed in the light, a wave of incredible fear swept through the audience and many older men clutched their chests. But it was not the black blood that stained the man's pitted cheeks, nor the oozing blisters and festering sores of suffocated skin that alarmed them. Nor was it the sweaty unkempt hair, matted and tangled about the ruined face, nor the feral eyes that looked out like those of the cornered rat; it was the memory of the war.

"He is the Executioner," a man gasped aloud. "The devil himself."

The truth of it spread like an evil fire until the entire audience understood that one of the most dangerous and ruthless persons to ever live stood before them. Heinrich recalled the story he'd heard told at the campfire and the nightmares that had followed. A woman sighed in the stands above him and slumped over in a faint, and he tried to not do the same.

The Executioner let loose a tremulous cry as blood streamed down his now naked face,

"I am the ghastly legend; and it is true, everything you've heard,
It is I, the one who wildly wasted lives. I am the Executioner!
The Great One did not know it, he never saw my face,
But now you see it and I beg you look at what's become of my disgrace!

I served the war with a blood rage. As I fought, everything went red,
And since that time I have cried these tears to remind me of the dead.
So I recall my violence and the many who are slain
And so I should never return to my wicked ways again.

Behold . . . I did abandon my ways . . . Oh but now, I wonder why!
Evil has killed the ones I love, and I've stood idly by.
I cannot let this happen. I no longer care, for now I see,
I can't become what the Great One believed that I could be."

The Executioner wiped strands of tangled hair from his face as he turned to Rabar. He drew a broadsword from his waist and challenged,

"Fight me Rabar, now you know my face and know my name,
I challenge you to fight with one who truly is ashamed!"

The crowd anxiously huddled together trying to stave off the plague of fear that swirled in the tent, but strangely, Rabar stood his ground and watched, seeming entertained and even amused. Deep in his scowl one might have even noticed the corners of his cruel mouth curl upwards. He snorted in contempt and turned away from the threats of the Executioner. Facing the crowd, he raised his own sword triumphantly, and called,

"Do you see? Do you now see what terror I expose?
See that I am right, these are wolves in human clothes!"

Though Rabar was horrible, the crowd reluctantly considered that he may be the lesser of two evils, and perhaps they would have to accept him as their champion. They made the sad choice of allowing one enemy to threaten another, exactly as the haunted veterans had first done with the Executioner in the war. Rabar finally readied his saber to answer the challenge, faced the Executioner and taunted,

"Show me what you can do, show me how you fight.
The more you show, the more you'll know that I am right!
You see, you are just like me, you know that life is cruel,
Man cannot escape his nature, no matter what he strives to do.

But, we can fight it and we can hide it, as you know we must,
Suffering, shame, and forced restraint are the truths we trust.
Fight me! Without your mask, you prove what I have claimed,
Man's is a wicked nature. It needs to be restrained!"

The Executioner gnashed his teeth and beat his sword against his thighs. The blood from his eyes was all the more horrifying without the mask. His rage burst in a roar and he charged, his broadsword crashing into Rabar's saber with a deafening ring.

As the crowd watched the duel through trembling fingers, Heinrich fretted. *I should never have returned to this place. Perhaps I can live haunted just as I've lived with the rest of my disappointing life.* At this moment, however, a movement in the shadows at the side of the arena caught his eye. The Great Mephisto's chest appeared to shudder.

Though he doubted his eyes, a small hope flickered in Heinrich. It was possible that the Great Mephisto was not mortally wounded. If the Great Mephisto was still alive, even if only for a moment, he might yet be able to do something about the destruction that had now befallen the circus. He recalled his helplessness when his father was stuck in the collapsed mine. He had not been able to do anything and was told no one could mount a rescue without causing another collapse. The days of agony, knowing his father was alive, and dying, and being unable to speak to him, still scarred him. He had only been able to wait and try to block

it from his mind. *He is still buried in that deep tomb to this day. Trapped like the dead butterfly in its chrysalis.*

Before he knew what he was doing, Heinrich snuck from underneath the stands and edged unnoticed towards the arena. As he crept forward, he silently urged, *Don't die, I need answers,* as if he could ask this dying hero what he could not ask his dying father. He recalled his father's letter and wondered, *What made you think I would do great things?* The Great Mephisto's chest inflated the slightest fraction of an inch. He was not gone! Heinrich's heart pounded in his chest, he ducked and crawled toward the body. The ring of steel striking steel reminded him that the two most terrifying men he'd ever seen were in a brutal battle only a few yards away. He could not believe he had entered the arena. Arriving at the prostrate body, he gripped the Great Mephisto's blood-stained collar and dragged him as far as he could into the shadows before he stopped, panting.

"Are you there?" he whispered.

Though blood saturated his shirt from a singed hole in the center of his chest, a mortal wound if ever there was one, the Great Mephisto's eyes fluttered open, but they did not focus on Heinrich. He motioned weakly for Heinrich to let him loose. He strained to lift his head and squinted, looking across the arena, ignoring the fighting men, only to discover the Mermaid sprawled out in the dirt, and he began to tremble until Heinrich was afraid he would be lost again. Heinrich whispered urgently, "You are alive . . . there is hope! You are alive!"

The action in the center of the arena was so great that no one paid attention to Heinrich and the Great Mephisto. Indeed, the Executioner stormed and attacked, he slashed as his scarlet cape swirled from his back. The crowd trembled, nervous and frightened, frantic with tensions heightened, and Rabar kept roaring for the Executioner to fight him. Hate came forth with rage and spite. Teeth flew to the ground, and sweat poured out to grease the fight, and flesh was lost as flesh was found.

Rabar faltered. The Executioner was far too powerful an opponent. Dripping with sweat and catching his breath, Rabar dropped to one knee.

The Executioner stood over him and effortlessly tossed his broadsword back and forth between his hands. Rabar spat out a tooth, glared up and hissed,

"Go ahead and kill me, beat me like a brute,
But feel your rage and know, I have already broken you!
You've lost all control, I've made you hate again.
If you destroy me, I'll be gone, but you . . . You will not win!"

Infuriated, the Executioner stepped towards Rabar and raised his sword, but stopped short of delivering the final blow. It was as though Rabar's words had cut him and he was now crippled by the wound.

In the shadows, the Great Mephisto gasped for air. His weary eyes settled on Heinrich, who had just spoken to him of hope. He deeply suffered the loss of the Mermaid, more even than his wound. He looked confused at Heinrich and said,

" You think I can make things right? Even now, you wish to see what I will do?
Can't you see? ***I've done it all! I've shaken the whole world up for you!"***

"What?" Heinrich asked, thunderstruck and worried that the man was not all there. "What did you do?" he insisted. His face screwed up in turmoil and tears began to run down his face. "What do mean you have shaken the world up for me?!"

The Great Mephisto choked, but then forced a whisper that wrenched at Heinrich's soul,

"I saw it in you when you were born, I see it in everything,
You, my son, are great; you will do great things."

Upon hearing the very same words his father had written, words he knew by heart and which no other living person knew, Heinrich felt like the air had been knocked out of him by a blow from a sledgehammer.

He gripped the Great Mephisto's collar tighter and searched the dying man's eyes desperately. *How could you know those words?* Then, as he looked closer at the man's face, every pore and wrinkle became crisp and focused. Those eyes, the long nose, the beard that pointed in two directions. The answer came rushing up at him and struck like a second hammer blow, and his body went cold and numb. He had seen that face before. It was the face of the hobo from the camp. The hobo who had told him about the train. The hobo that had returned his jacket. The Great Mephisto and the hobo were one and the same.

"You read my letter!" he gasped, still trying to understand how he had not recognized the hobo before. The Great Mephisto nodded.

"But he was wrong. Don't you see?" Heinrich insisted. "I am not great. I have no idea what I should do." The Great Mephisto's eyes cleared and blazed with light for a moment,

"Yet here you are in the midst of a battle, trying to understand,
I once whipped a helpless soul, yet I am a champion of man!
For I still see a bright future, though my vision is going black,
Don't ever let your pain or disappointment hold you back.

Your father wrote true, you will soon see how he was right!
You took his promise as your burden, but his was faith in life.
He saw it when you were born because he saw that life is good,
If you accept that, then you are great. That's what needs be understood!"

Kneeling under the light illuminating the center of the arena, Rabar peered up at the Executioner's hesitation, and chuckled with surprise,

"Aha, you see! You do not kill me, and I will reason why,
You hope I keep on fighting and you are the one to die!"

The Executioner's sword lowered a fraction as though it had become too heavy, and in that hesitation, Rabar sprung up and positioned his sword at the Executioner's neck. Strangely, the Executioner did not counter or move back. With a look of utter disdain, Rabar said,

"You should have stayed locked up behind your mask,
Where you hid yourself, where you refrained to act.
Now you cannot hide, and you must pay your toll,
Do as you would have done before Mephisto 'saved' your soul.

The Great Mephisto is a liar, his words have lost their power,
There is only one option left, so do it yourself you coward!"

The Executioner's arms dropped and hung limply at his sides, defeated. His breastplate looked hollow and empty. He dropped to the ground, bashing his knees on the dirt. Apathetically, he raised his broadsword up, the sharp point angled down, and tilted his head back. The audience covered their eyes and those of their innocent, desperately hoping, despite all they had seen, that what would follow might only be a sword swallowing act. The Executioner or not, they did not have the stomachs to see his suicide. Rabar hollered as the Executioner's blade tilted into position,

"Yes! Do it! Answer for your wicked past,
A violent end to a violent man. Show that justice comes at last.
Do it, murderer, do it! In this world, you have no place!
End your suffering, give it up! End your horrible disgrace!"

A crack of lightning struck so close to the tent that the thunder immediately shook the walls. Rabar's voice rose to a fever pitch,

"All your choices are destructive, go ahead and lower down the blade!
Witness all, the great folly of man, he was so poorly made!"

Upon hearing Rabar say this, the Bearded Lady was stirred from her self-pity and raised her hairy head for the first time since she'd seen the Great Mephisto shot. She wiped away the tears and makeup that blurred her vision. A flash in the arena attracted her and she focused on it like a hawk. When it dawned on her what she was seeing, her faith and determination returned full force and she became truly wild.

Heinrich, made oblivious to the drama in the center of the arena by the revelations of the dying circus leader, saw that the Great Mephisto/hobo was as flawed and simple as himself, except that he had forgiven himself and held no shame about who he was or his cruel and troublesome past. Seeing the man's face humbled by death's approach, Heinrich finally understood how it could be that this man was so incredibly great and also only a ragged hobo in the dirt, just as the circus was wonderful and also very terrible. Neither aspect was better than the other. He understood that life could be both a disappointment and also the greatest triumph at the same time. Heinrich realized that he needed to accept all the aspects of life, including the pain, and move forward, trusting it was good. He no longer wished to run away.

The Great Mephisto relaxed as though he'd found something he'd been searching for, like the light at the end of a tunnel. He cast a final look upon the Mermaid sprawled out on the other side of the arena, and whispered cryptically,

> *"Our act is done, my love, but I have enjoyed the play,*
> *Do not despair, just watch, love will yet win out this day."*

He looked to Heinrich again and smiled through his tears as he forced a final whisper,

> *"Now, I can do nothing more, but let me tell you so it's all made clear,*
> *I have **already** saved us all . . . I sent that train, I brought **you** here!*
> *And now maybe you realize, this is the part where you go alone,*
> *Out there, Heinrich, is the fire . . . the fire and the roughest stone!"*

XXXIX Suicide

The Great Mephisto's eyes closed and his expression softened. Heinrich clenched his teeth as a grief gripped his heart. He was too distraught to wonder how the Great Mephisto had found him and sent a train for him. It did not matter now. As he held the body, the pain and angst from his father's death surged back to him and stirred up his fears and disappointments in himself, but for once, he let them flow through him. The Great Mephisto found abandoned people, and Heinrich had been one—abandoned by himself. Then a calm blossomed in him and his mind cleared. He gently laid the dead man down and had an idea as to how the Great Mephisto's bringing him to the circus would indeed save them all.

He understood that he was indeed a part of the life that both the Great Mephisto and his father had placed their faith in. The pressure he'd felt to become something great was not real. His great future was not his father's expectation, it was his father's trust that life was good. Heinrich realized he had nothing to prove, and everything to reveal. He did not have to change himself, he had to accept himself, and he was no longer afraid to do so. Like the caterpillar who enters the chrysalis, he would trust something greater than himself, let go and become his truth. He saw that there was real magic in the truth, and understood that the performers in the circus, all the stories he had heard, were very real and very true. He understood that to live greatly is to live an honest life, and that to do so was the greatest gift one could both give and enjoy. Filled with forgiveness and gratitude, he resolved, *I accept it all. That is what it means to live a life.*

The flash that had attracted the Bearded Lady/Mary came from the sword held vertically by the Masked Man who was no longer wearing his iron helmet. The face of the Masked Man, which she had not seen, and which caused the audience such horror, caused her to tremble with joy. He was none other than her Ulysses. Why Ulysses knelt in the center of the arena with a sword poised above his head, she did not immediately understand and would never care. She leapt to her feet like one who jolts awake from a nightmare and every muscle fiber in her body tensed. A cry of joy escaped her and she clasped her hands to her face, then pulled them away as quickly, discovering strands of hair caught in her fingers. She brought her hands to her face again and pulled them away with the same effect. Her vision blurred anew as she realized her beard had fallen away along with her grief. She raced into the arena more wild than the cavewoman she had pretended to be and screamed,

> *"Stop it! Stop at once! You fool! Draw back that blade!*
> *You owe a debt of love that has far too long been left unpaid!"*

She leapt at Ulysses, and rocketing through the air above him, delivered a flying kick that sent his broadsword flying from his hands. Rabar jumped back in shock. Mary landed, and ignoring Rabar, towered over Ulysses. She raised her hands in determined fists and went wild,

> *"What do you think you're doing? Have you forgotten who you used to be?*
> *Did you forget that there are two? The other half of you is me!*
> *I never gave up hope for you and I never will, despite your misery,*
> *You may give up on yourself, but I'll not let you give up on me!"*

Seeing the wife he had abandoned because he was too ashamed to return home, forgive him, as he had never been able to, Ulysses began to break down. He looked at her like one might look upon an angel from the heavens and managed to mutter, in the most mystified, yet grateful tone,

"How . . . how could you?"

And for the first time since the war, clear tears flowed from his eyes and washed the blood from his cheeks.

The Executioner's/Ulysses' broadsword settled in the dust near Heinrich. He glanced over at it and a gleam in the blade reminded him of the gypsy's curtained cabinet. Suddenly, he understood what the face that haunted him was, as he accepted its truth along with that of the rest of the circus, as he had recognized the Great Mephisto for the hobo, and he realized how to stop Rabar.

"So that it is all made plain," he whispered and he grabbed the hilt of the sword.

XL She Went Wild

Chapter IX
Heinrich Speaks

Rabar looked horrified and bewildered by the reunion of Mary and Ulysses, and that Mary, the Bearded Lady, no longer had a beard. He was furious that the sword had been kicked out of Ulysses' hand and he remained alive. Outside, the fury of the storm grew as though matching his mood. The tent poles creaked and the canvas flapped like the sails of a tall ship in a hurricane. A lightning bolt cracked across the sky, momentarily blinding and deafening everyone in the tent. Rabar rushed at the unarmed couple, raised his foot and shoved his heeled boot into Mary's back. She slammed into Ulysses and the two sprawled in the dirt. Rabar screamed in a tantrum,

"How dare you! You do not deserve love, love is not a game to play,
You don't give it to the undeserving. How dare you tarnish love this way!
Love is for the good people, not for the likes of you nor I,
How dare you believe this man should live. Of all men, he deserves to die!
Look at the pain he caused you, why will you not listen?
You are only asking to suffer more, he cannot be forgiven!"

Rabar stomped his boot on Ulysses' chest and raised his sword. Ulysses put his arm around Mary and said,

"You may swing your sword, but you have already missed,
For all your murderous hate, you could never defeat this."

Rabar gripped his sword more firmly, prepared to make the final cut, and yelled to the audience,

"He is the Executioner! If you allow this, you are all to blame,
Understand you simple minded fools . . ."

But he was interrupted by a voice that rang out as boldly as a lone cricket's song,

"You should never be ashamed!"

Rabar spun around wildly. Heinrich was standing in front of him and leveling the Executioner's sword at his chest. When Rabar saw this, he scoffed,

"Who is this that steals my thunder? A simple man from town?
Run back to the stands young man and put that silly weapon down!"

But Heinrich stood fast, absolute and unflinching like a freight train. A bright gleam shone in his eyes.

"I'll not put it down and I will not take my seat,
For in this sword, I swear, I will show you your defeat."

Rabar balked, incredulous and curious. A sneer scrawled over his face, and he replied,

"How you speak, indeed. But why am I surprised!
Are you the town madman? Is that your 'disguise?'
In any case, please go on. Have the stage and let us hear,
What other insane madness Mephisto has inspired here."

He exaggerated a mocking bow and stepped back offering up the spotlight. Unexpectedly, Heinrich bowed deeply to Rabar with the sincerest respect. He entered the circle of light and spoke to Rabar unafraid,

> *"'Why would the Great One let you in?' I asked. 'Why are you here?'*
> *It is so we know you, and know you are not someone to fear.*
> *So we can accept you, and all you do, just as he has done,*
> *And learn any truths about ourselves that we have hidden from.*
>
> *So, Captain Rabar I thank you, I now see as I never would have dared,*
> *I am one of the legion lost and it is you who should beware!*
> *Do you now wonder who I am and what part do I play?*
> *Behold, I am the most frightening man to ever set foot upon this stage!*
>
> *You do not know my face. You do not know my name,*
> *And for that, I fear, you have only myself to blame . . ."*

The audience leaned in. There was nothing special about Heinrich, with his dusty slacks, sweat stained shirt, and suspenders, except just that; he looked extremely ordinary, and yet was doing an extremely unordinary

thing. For the first time since the rumblings of the storm began, they subsided, and Heinrich's voice rang out, fragile and terrific,

> *"Tragedy once struck my life, I lost one who believed in me,*
> *Before he saw who I might become, or who I might be.*
> *I did not want to move on and fail, so I abandoned my fate,*
> *I thought his faith had been misplaced, I was never great.*
>
> *So I escaped from life, I reasoned I wasn't ready.*
> *I blamed the past and rejected any future that seemed unsteady.*
> *I waited for things to come, I slowly let life slip by,*
> *I did not want to do it wrong and was too afraid to try.*
> *I judged life a disappointment, so I gave up, this is my sin!*
> *I forsook myself! I am the man that would have never been!"*

Heinrich began to tremble as he strode. He lifted the broadsword above his head and continued,

> *"I was found in the wayward plains where I tried to cheat this life,*
> *To look away when dreams were lost and hopes were left to die.*
> *But now I now accept a reality I long struggled to admit,*
> *Life does not hide from us; it is we who hide from it!*
>
> *Look around! This show is wasted, but it did not have to be,*
> *Before this pirate cast his doubts, we enjoyed the revelry.*
> *But the cheers quickly vanished, though I am not surprised,*
> *I too abandoned the wonder I saw right before my eyes.*
> *We've let another fill our thoughts with angst instead of awe,*
> *How quickly we forget life's glory; Let me tell you what I saw!*
>
> *I saw a giant dance in ways I could never have expected,*
> *And now I wonder what else my prejudice has rejected.*

I saw an animated doll, though small and made of wood,
Dance because he could not, not because he could!

I saw a singing maiden, with a spirit so bold and true,
She let me hear a song, I would never have listened to.

I saw a lady, cursed and tired, love so resolutely,
That, despite her appearance, I witnessed real beauty.

And I saw a man accept love though he'd been ravaged by war,
Forgiveness is more powerful than anything I have ever seen before."

Heinrich pointed the broadsword at Rabar again.

"And you, Rabar, who sought destruction when you came swinging in,
You believed you'd end it all, but this is where the show begins!
Though another man who believed in me lies dead, I now understand,
It was not me, but in this life, those men were invested in.
Life is so much grander than anything you or I could do,
At last, may I accept it and let this life shine through."

The darkness in the tent ebbed. Heinrich took a step toward Rabar and said,

"Like the Great Mephisto I have many truths, but I refused to see them,
My shames were trapped too long inside because I refused to free them!"

Rabar stepped back as though taking Heinrich as a serious threat, but Heinrich stepped up face to face with him. Rabar cringed as if he were watching a corpse crawl from a grave, but Heinrich continued to close the space between them. He brought the Executioner's sword between their two faces and angled the blade so Rabar could see Heinrich's reflection in it. Heinrich whispered,

"I am potential unheeded. I am the unsatisfied fate denied!
I've not done evil things . . . I've done nothing . . . And look what that's
done to me inside!"

Rabar looked at the reflection in the blade and his face turned ashen, and he staggered back. Heinrich slowly turned so the audience too could see his reflection in the sword. It was now their turn to quail before the face that had come to haunt Heinrich. They recoiled back from the image, for it was a gaunt head with stringy hair, peeling skin, and exposed muscle and bone. Its yellow, veined eyes and tortured grimace moved at the same time, and in the same directions, as Heinrich's features. He explained to the crowd,

"I am not wicked or dangerous, that's not why I am damned,
I rotted away because I mistrusted fate, I never took a chance!
What if I tried and failed? I worried. How would I escape?
Would I be trapped for all to see, dead at the final stage?
But here I am upon this stage, the final act for all to see,
I have failed, I tried hiding, I am not great. This is me!"

Rabar quailed and cried out,

"I don't understand. How could your soul look so vile?
You are not strange. I never thought to put you on trial!"

Heinrich answered,

"I would never have let you, for I was too afraid,
Instead of being judged, I would have run away.

And you are like I was, you doubt the hand of fate,
You think it dealt you poorly, so you fight it with your hate,
You see, we run and fight because we are so afraid,
That we have nothing to offer; that we are poorly made!"

Rabar continued to stare at Heinrich's ghastly reflection moving as
he spoke, and could not reply. Heinrich challenged,

"The Great Mephisto did not fight and did not run away,
He was here to accept and learn, and find a better way.
But you won the day; he and the others are destroyed,
But now I stand before you and you cannot fight a void!

So forget how you might prove your worth, do not fit a mold,
Discover and accept yourself. Let a truth unfold!
Reveal to us a truth that has never been defined,
Who were you made to be? What is your design?"

The tent became lighter and at the same time, a light patter of rain
began. Heinrich swept the Executioner's sword above his head and called
at the quivering Rabar as though calling out a demon,

"Reveal yourself. Look at me, I will not be afraid!
I will not run! Stop your fighting! Reveal how you were made!

Know me now, I am imperfect, and it is because I falter,
That I see a greater power and it has everything to offer!
It will shine through me as I accept the reflection in this blade,
This is the glory of man . . . He is poorly made!"

At this moment the sun broke through the clouds and a deluge poured over the tent and the people were treated to the rare wonder of rain as the sun shines. The rain was so great that a dripping through the tear in the roof that Rabar had rent larger, grew into a heavy waterfall and poured into the arena. Mist from the crashing water swirled into a light beam shining through the tear and created a scintillating rainbow that arched across the tent. Heinrich intercepted the rainbow with his broadsword and reflected the rainbow's colors to every corner of the tent. Blazing violets, emerald greens, lemon yellows, and ruby reds dazzled the crowd, and Heinrich began radiating with a brilliant golden light. Then, the Spirit of the Universe resounded from his mouth, and said,

"You show me myself: I am the light that burns in you,
My colors are revealed by your soul as I shine through!
Each person is vital; you reveal my spectrum's range,
This life formed you perfectly, this life is The Fantastic Strange!

Ask not that it be good to you, it makes you to be kind,
Remain alive and honest, and endure it with an open mind.
Be the one that accepts the most, and honor all you meet,
And your greatness be in what you show, not what you defeat.
Do not chide how others shine, celebrate their gain,
Do not ever fear your light, let it be made plain!
Let this echo in your ears, here I live, and here I thrive!
Take joy in your existence. That is what it means to be alive!"

XLI The Spirit Of The Universe

Chapter X
So Much Wonder

Rabar covered his eyes and ears from the sound and radiance emanating from Heinrich, and did as Heinrich once would have done. Leaping through the muddy puddles, he ran away. No one watched him go, being too distracted by Heinrich and the brilliant colors flashing around the tent. The pouring waterfall had begun to fill the arena like a pool and as the level of the water raised, Tack's body floated and a current swept him through the performer's exit. Then, to everyone's surprise, a small girl from the crowd squealed,

"The Mermaid is alive!"

Everyone looked at once. The Mermaid's tail kicked in three inches of water. She raised herself up with shaking arms. Heinrich, uncertain of what had just happened to him and incredulous to what was happening, let go of the broadsword, fainted and fell over backward.

The Mermaid, reviving, immediately looked for the Great Mephisto's body and zeroing in on it, she half swam, half crawled across the arena, dragging herself like a baby turtle pushing itself over dunes of sand to the sea. She collapsed on his body, put her webbed hands on either side of his face and kissed his lips as she had once done, for the first time, on a very distant shore so long ago. As before, Mephisto breathed. The audience surged from their seats. With the Mermaid's help, the Great Mephisto stood and applause erupted from the stands. The rain abated and the late afternoon sun blazed into the tent.

After nodding to his love, the Great Mephisto ran to the fainted Heinrich, grabbed him by the shoulders, lifted him up and shook him. Heinrich's eyes opened and his heart began to beat like a giant bass drum in his chest. Cheers echoed around the two men louder than the thunder had ever been and seemed like they would never stop. The Great Mephisto smiled and cried,

> *"Thank you for who you are! You are perfect unrestrained.*
> *Welcome to life dear Heinrich! Welcome to The Fantastic Strange!*

The Great Mephisto turned to the crowd with the vigor of a man who has never been shot. The blood stain on his shirt had washed away. He pointed at the tear in the roof of the tent just as he had done when dressed as a hobo, and shouted,

> *"And now we finish very much like we began,*
> *You once regarded me as just an aimless man.*
> *I pointed out that tear. Then Rabar tore it open,*
> *Celebrate your flaws! They let the wonder in!"*

The Great Mephisto gathered the Mermaid into his arms and stood with Mary and Ulysses. They clasped hands to make a bow, but Heinrich did not join. He had left the tent.

ACT FOUR
After The Show

Chapter I
Gold

Heinrich, who was now willing to accept anything, hoped everyone who had died at the circus might come back to life. He'd left the bigtop to search for Medina and now found the circus grounds in shambles. Several caravans lay on their sides, and stages and tents had collapsed in the storm. Nonetheless, he found muddy footprints he believed the Masked Man/Ulysses had made when he'd carried Medina from the show, and followed them until he heard a wail from behind a tent. He peered around a corner and spied none other than Rabar sprawled in muddy grass between two tents. The rain had let up, but hot tears streamed down Rabar's face. He was panting and a tooth fell from his mouth in a stream of saliva. He picked it out of the mud and examined it. Holes speckled the surface of the tooth and dark yellow stains marked the roots. He threw it away and despaired,

> *"What happened? How could that man have been so bold?*
> *He should have been brought down, he should have been controlled.*
> *They should have listened to me, why will people not confess,*
> *They have wicked ways and they need to be suppressed?"*

He raised his face to the retreating clouds.

> *"People are not good because they forgive their imperfections,*
> *But let them glorify their faults, I will be the grand exception!*
> *The day will come when they admit I had the better plan,*
> *For I will fix the cracks in me, I'll not be a broken man."*

Rabar looked down as a bright glow radiating from under the wall of a tent captured his attention. He wiped the tears from his face, scurried across the grass and peered under the tent wall. Suddenly, he slithered under the wall, into the tent. Heinrich hurried over, knelt down, and lifted up the canvas just enough to peek in. Rabar was crawling on his hands and knees amongst an incredible treasure. Dark weathered chests overflowed with precious stones including diamonds, sapphires, emeralds, and rubies. Chalices stood amongst the chests and spilled over with golden coins. Strings of pearls draped over silver figurines, marble statuettes, and golden lamps. Tattered scrolls stuck out of vases and leather tomes piled on each other in stacks four feet high. Rabar drooled and muttered to himself,

> *"This is all my treasure, alas, it's been used to fund a circus.*
> *It ends here, I will take it all and throw it in a furnace."*

Heinrich stayed outside the tent and kept an eye on Rabar to ensure he would not escape. Rabar picked up a small ring with a stone carved as the face of the moon. Suddenly, a light from the far side of the tent caused the moonstone to flash a brilliant blue and a long shadow fell over Rabar. Then his arm jerked forward as a knife pinned his cuff to a wooden chest. He spun around only to have a second blade pierce the cuff of his other sleeve and sink with a shudder into a barrel full of rubies. He tried to jerk his wrists free only to have three more blades pin down his long coat on both sides of his body. Rabar snarled and looked up. Heinrich followed his gaze and almost fainted again.

Medina stood at the entrance of the tent, a sunset of rose colors backlighting her tall figure. She twirled a knife in one hand and said,

"I do not miss when I throw my blades,
For I learned too well in an evil trade,
And though that was ever so long ago,
I remember how I became deadly, and I recall the cretin that made me so.

I sensed you coming, you dark unwelcomed guest,
I knew you'd arrived when a blade went through my chest.
How disappointing, you took your stab when I was fettered,
But really I am honored that you even remembered."

Rabar kicked his heels in the ground, trying to push himself back, and thrashed side to side. When he settled down, he said between heavy breaths,

"Then you have me to thank, and owe a debt you lying tart,
If it was aboard my ship you learned your deadly art."

Medina gripped the knife she twirled and her voice rose,

"The art of hiding who I was, letting a beautiful life become defiled,
It is you who owe the debt of my deadly loss when I was just a child!

I owe you nothing, save your wicked breath,
When you discovered who I was, you sent me down to death."

Rabar smiled.

"Ahh, but I was not the only one,
Poor Victor saw what you'd become.
I just gave you both what he preferred,
An escape from all you'd ruined, to avoid living as you were."

At this, Medina faltered for a fraction of a second. The knife slipped from her fist. She caught it up quickly, suffering a slice on her finger. Rabar took the opportunity of her distraction and pressed a small spring at his wrist. A tiny pistol pushed from his sleeve, into his hand, and he aimed it at Medina,

"My dear, I don't know how you've tricked your fate,
But I have much to do and your hour has grown too late."

Medina, perceiving Rabar's pistol, let out a high pitched laugh. She twirled on her toes and replied,

"You fool, go ahead and try,
Shoot your pistol, I shall not die!
Don't you wonder about this crooked dance with Death I play?
My first step was on your plank, 'twas you that made me dance this way!

You already killed me once; I'm no longer on the reaper's list,
He no longer looks for me; Death knows not that I exist.
You see, when I was drowning, Victor gave me his last breath,
I gave to him my heart, so he took two hearts down to Death.

Victor takes care that my wicked heart does not go to hell.

XLII Gold

And I remain alive, though I am just an empty shell.
I stand before you, Judge, the outcome of your cruelty,
By destroying who I was, you fool, you created me!"

Rabar pulled the trigger, but there was no deadly blast. Only a faint
fizzle sounded before a mere trace of smoke eked from the gun barrel.
Medina hardly even noticed Rabar's sad attempt. Instead, she closed her
eyes and raised her chin as though she sensed something. Her head moved
back and forth like a snake flicking its tongue and picking up a scent. Suddenly, her eyes sprang open and she focused directly on Heinrich peeking
under the tent. He was caught spying on her again! She nodded at him with
a knowing look and hurled a blade straight toward his face. Just as before,
it was not meant to harm him. The knife pierced the canvas right in front
of his nose and pinned it to the ground so he could look on no more.

The Giant sat shaking in the shade of a battered stage. Streams of rain-water flowed past his large feet and soaked his pants. A small object upstream dislodged from a clump of grass and floated on the current until it bumped into his ankle. He looked down and found it to be his dear little friend, Master Tack. He picked up the lifeless doll and closed his large sad eyes as his head swung side to side, then held still for a moment. In a burst of energy, the Giant surged to his feet and raised Master Tack into the air. As though continuing a conversation that had been going on in his mind, the Giant said,

> *"Little helpless man, you never feared me at all,*
> *When who out there, more than me, could make you feel small?*
> *But at the foot of a giant you demanded, 'Look at me!'*
> *I learned from you that living large is to do it gratefully."*

The Giant's massive fist tightened around Master Tack's body. He released a terrible yell that shook the tents at his feet. When he let up, his grip loosened, and he looked at the horizon with his shoulders slumped forward and he sighed. At that moment a small voice piped up,

> *"Yell louder, Giant! To learn is to live, that is what it is about,*
> *It stands to reason you are not living if you have it figured out!"*

A smile opened the Giant's face revealing his lopsided teeth behind his long mustache. Master Tack stood up on the Giant's palm and busily flicked mud off his wooden arms. The Giant placed Master Tack on his shoulder, spread out his arms and yelled so loud the sun set, casting its final ray on a man who lived greatly despite having nothing, and a man who'd become great despite having so much regret.

Epilogue

The following morning found the train engine already chugging and blowing smoke, ready to depart. The circus had been dismantled and stowed in the various vehicles it had arrived in. All the stakes and trash had been collected and the field looked much like it had before the circus arrived, excepting the green sprouts that had already started to grow from the previous day's rain.

Many of the townsfolk, all of whom had gone home the previous evening in absolute amazement, and many of whom had not been able to sleep they'd been so excited, now wandered the grounds in hopes they could meet some of the players and relive a little of the show's magic. They wanted to see the performers out of costume and congratulate them on their performances. As for the Executioner, the townsfolk had determined that he must have been only a look-a-like, in costume like the rest. They wondered if they might meet the man who had choreographed the entire spectacle, he who played the part of the Great Mephisto, as well as the actor who played the ordinary man, Heinrich, as his performance had been so convincing. A few were curious to see the Mermaid walking around without her costume, as they had already seen what the Bearded Lady looked like without her beard and that had been fun. Alas, the players were no longer there and the people, not having expected the show to leave so quickly, felt the pangs of a vacancy where there had been so much life just a day before.

However, standing alone in the field, one display had not yet been stowed; one final exhibit remained. Medina's target stood propped up in the mud and a vulture perched on its top edge. On the front of the target, Rabar hung, pinned by seven blades through his clothes. Above his head, a sign read, "Murderer." Rabar was still in costume and in character; still terribly ugly and wavering between seething rage and tears of anguished hopelessness.

Most of the townsfolk walking by averted their gazes and hurried past. A group of young men laughed, knowing it was part of the show, but their laughs proved uneasy and soon trailed off. A small child with two thick chestnut braids and a yellow calico dress, stopped before the display. She tilted her head sideways and curiously watched Rabar hiss and moan. She alone took a dainty step toward him and placed a hand-picked bouquet of blue cornflowers at his feet. Straightening back up, she looked into his yellow eyes. She smiled, shyly tucked her chin back and said,

"You are fantastic."

The End

XLIII Judgment

About the Author

Daniel (Danny) Von der Ahe is a painter who is always creating, taking notes, and observing the world around him and the thoughts that pass through his head. He believes that with focused energy and time most things are possible, and so he gives it, vigorously, to the multitude of passions that overwhelm him, and feels fortunate to be able to do so. This is his first novel. He has several more in the works and will begin writing the next after a break and a great deal of oil painting.

For more information about this novel and the art inside, and links to other projects Danny is working on, visit: thefantasticstrange.com

*"May it be that I am the human champion,
the one that believed in us the very most."*

Acknowledgements

This labor of love, which seemed to come out of nowhere, had instrumental support readily emerge to bolster it along its strange way. What a gift. I would like to acknowledge the people who believed in and helped in this venture (even in its very awkward infant stages), who allowed it to become all that I wanted it to be and much more, and to whom I have a deep gratitude and respect.

I was told, and sadly admitted it might be true, that no one would care for my project as much as I did, but it was not so and two people did:

Kameron Campbell, my fiancé, for her undying support, faith, and optimism for this novel. She understood it all so immediately and breathed her unflagging energy into its completion.

Matt Brooks, who is an incredible friend, with whom I grew up in a way. Many of the conversations we had as we did so are the basis of the themes in this novel. I thank him for his support and insights which changed and strengthened significant points of this story for the better, and for his taking the time to consider this story with his genuine care.

To no lesser degree I acknowledge those that helped this book become a reality: Pat, for his recommendations, editing, and pointing the way to learn to write; Andy, Christy, Duck, and Spike, for their time and perseverance reading through the rough stages and providing invaluable feedback; and Chris, for his design and putting the multitudinous parts of this book together.

CPSIA information can be obtained
at www.ICGtesting.com
Printed in the USA
FSOW04n2256240317
32126FS